A
SEASON
OF
PEACE

A
SEASON
OF
PEACE

St. Martin's Press
New York

Library of Congress Cataloging-in-Publication Data

Armitage, G. E.
    A season of peace.

    I. Title.
PR6051.R563S43 1986   823′.914   86-1872
ISBN 0-312-70824-6

First published in Great Britain by Martin Secker & Warburg Limited.

First U.S. Edition

10 9 8 7 6 5 4 3 2 1

'I take it that what all men are really after is some form or perhaps only some formula of peace.'

Joseph Conrad: Prologue to *Under Western Eyes* Part I

For Sara

part one

one

I cannot explain it, but one of my strongest, most persistent memories of those final days at Cable Point is of the gull. I remember every detail of its apparently undamaged body hanging across the door, its hooked beak and black marble eyes level with my face, rain dripping from its free wing, gesturing as it swung. It was only as I took the bird down that I felt the looseness of its neck and saw the bruise where it had collided with the tower during the night.

The wing had caught in the mesh casing of a light above the door. I was able to dislodge it by pulling, feeling the feathers tense and then give as a bone broke and the bird fell at my feet. I remember being unaccountably anxious, frightened almost, that once free the gull might somehow miraculously revive and beat against me in its struggle to escape.

I gave the body to the children, all of them stroking and plucking at the white plumage before pulling the wings open and marching towards the sea in a brief, childishly formal ceremony.

It was Mary who explained that it was unusual to find a body in such good condition. Usually, she said, they had already been broken by the sea, picked at by the other birds, and rolled into sand-coated bags of grey feather and bone. Even the birds blown against the Light fell to the concrete base and were lost.

She stroked the bird's head as she spoke. Her small brother stood beside her, watching me anxiously, as though I might be about to reclaim the body for myself.

I remember also the women coming out of the terrace of houses, shouting to each other as they searched for any damage the previous night's storm might have inflicted upon their isolated and exposed homes. They were laughing, genuinely unconcerned, too accustomed to their way of life to believe any longer in their own power over what might happen to them. Behind them I heard the scrape of the waves against the shingle bank which fell between the houses and the sea. The storm had blown itself out in the darkness, and already the September sky was beginning to lose its colour. Steam rose from the whitewashed walls and from the lighthouse itself.

The small boy studied my face. I smiled in an effort to assure him that the gull was his, theirs. He looked from me to it, and then to his sister. Mary smiled directly at me and said nothing. Their mother shouted and the boy turned and ran towards her.

In the broken concrete and rusting mesh beyond the Light, the petrol-driven generators were started up, and the men disembarking from the covered lorries filled the silence with their shouting and laughter. They also began to search for signs of damage, lifting tarpaulins to examine machinery and tools, hoping perhaps that they would be unable to continue and that the day would be spent bathing or playing cards in hidden places amongst the half-demolished concrete structures. Mary looked past me, watching the small brown figures, already naked to the waist, as they moved over the open space. Several of them waved to her. She smiled, flattered by their attention. Even at fifteen, she had far more in common with them than she ever would with me.

The line of empty lorries waited beside the houses, ready to move over the uneven ground to where the piles of yesterday's rubble awaited removal from the site. On the cab doors and bonnets were the stencilled military insignia and the hand-painted names of the places they had been: places in North Africa, Italy, France, and Germany – names the rest of the country was doing its utmost to forget.

I knew for certain that once away from the site the drivers stopped, and that the time taken on each round trip was twice what it should have been. But they were still Army drivers, and so soon after the war there was a growing belief in their right to take such unaccustomed liberties. They spoke to me with nods instead of salutes, and I sensed their resentment at being detained, their eagerness to return to civilian life.

I heard them shouting to the women and children, and watched as they reached down to exchange cigarettes for hot drinks. There was something shabby about their lack of discipline and motivation, but still something slightly glamorous, I suppose, about their presence in that isolated place whose war had existed only in the fortifications we were there to destroy, in newspapers and radio broadcasts, in the precise formations of American bombers forming overhead, and in the distant trails of smoke as small convoys crossed the perfect horizon of the North Sea.

I had offered my apologies to the women, but they had only laughed and insisted that I did nothing to restrict the men, that they deserved their 'freedom'. In this way, too, I began to feel alienated.

I told Mary that she and the other children should leave the site. She turned abruptly and walked away, as though I had offended or insulted her. I wanted to shout after her and apologise. Instead, I watched as she moved along the line of lorries, flirting silently with the men, ignoring their gestures and comments. She turned to wave briefly in my direction before entering the door beside which her mother waited. The woman, too, raised her arm in an uncertain gesture. I waved, and the men in the lorries turned to look. The woman's arm fell and I realised that she had simply been shielding her eyes from the sun. She watched me before following her daughter indoors.

13

Why those few minutes between the discovery of the gull, the woman's gesture and the staring faces of the men should have returned so vividly, I cannot explain.

In the doorway Mary had paused and spoken to her mother. The woman cocked her head, her arms folded. Beside her, Mary had disappeared into the shadowed interior of their home. I remember it as though it might have been a spoiled photograph upon which the outline of the girl had been inadvertently superimposed from another frame.

I turned to the gull, watching it spin as the cord to which the children had tied its legs slowly unwound. And I remember touching it, pulling my hand away and causing them to burst into laughter and run towards the dunes, the bird being dragged along the ground behind them, its body bouncing, its wings opening and closing, as though it had finally revived and was making a last, pathetic attempt to escape.

Now, thirty-two years later, my own son is dead. Michael. Killed in Londonderry by a booby-trapped car which took both his feet, leaving him ten days to live, his legs amputated below the knee, still mercifully unconscious when he died. He was twenty-eight, an only child, and his death has filled our home with unspoken regrets and raging silences.

Behind me I hear her move her newspaper, but I know she is not reading, simply going through the motions, striving to return to a normality neither of us will achieve. She will hold the folded paper close to her face and I will hear it shake. Occasionally she will turn the page. When she wants to cry she goes upstairs or into another room and I hear her through the walls.

Tomorrow his body is being flown home, three days after his death. I will drive to the military airfield and sign the papers for its release, guiding the van in which it will be carried to our home. We will bury him the following day. I have insisted on a private ceremony, declining the military honours offered.

Whilst he was still alive, she had been to visit him, returning with the assurance that when he regained consciousness he would be returned home. She was already planning his discharge from the Army. In the hospital they had been optimistic about his chances of adapting to life with artificial limbs. He was still young and this, they had explained, would work in his favour. She repeated everything they had told her – partly to console herself and partly to challenge my own unexpressed opinions. She had brought with her some brochures illustrating artificial hands and legs, arms and articulated fingers; photographs of smiling men on whom the unnaturally glossy devices were supposedly barely noticeable. Nothing was said of his chances of recovery, and three days after her return he had died.

An officer and uniformed padre had arrived, and I had watched without speaking as she, certain that they were there to initiate proceedings for his return, had insisted on giving them tea and telling them of the support he would receive, of the plans she had made. After a while she understood the true purpose of their visit and left the room. Neither of the men spoke, but their anxiety showed in their eyes and the padre smiled nervously, waiting for my attention before slowly shaking his head. I let them know I understood and left them.

I held her firmly and said simply that Michael had died, confirming what she already knew, but needed to hear me say. For a minute there was nothing: the silence of stunned grief broken eventually by the rising whistle of the kettle and then by her own convulsive crying.

I took her upstairs and returned to the waiting men. I eased the situation by outlining my own service history. The details were unimportant: I spoke simply to break the silence and to cover the sound of her crying. As I spoke, they relaxed, as though the shock of my son's death no longer existed between us; as though their discomfort had been an act for our benefit. I disappointed them both by once again refusing their offer of a military burial.

They left, and the house became full of the sound of her

crying, her face pressed into a pillow, the sound soaking through the walls to where I sat and waited.

The anti-aircraft battery was established at Cable Point in the winter of '42–3. It was intended as a defensive measure against the expected bombing raids on the sprawling American air bases being constructed inland.

The raids never materialised on the scale expected, and from the documentary evidence alone it appeared that the battery had been most effective in providing protection for the small, unescorted convoys of merchantmen moving up and down the East Coast.

On several occasions since the demolition of the site, I have met Army and Navy officers who remember the battery and lighthouse as important landmarks on their precarious journeys. The records of the battery boast of the destruction of eleven enemy aircraft, only nine of which were ever officially confirmed.

During my first visit in November 1942, the families of the keeper and coastguards had been evacuated, the isolated terrace of houses standing as they had been left, planks nailed across the doors. The lighthouse, too, had been rendered unusable for the duration – a strange move, the purpose of which I never understood.

I remember quite clearly watching the drums of grey and brown paint being delivered with which the brilliantly white structure was to be camouflaged. The task was never carried out and the drums remained unopened over three years later when I returned to supervise the demolition of the site.

Some of the containers had succumbed to the salt air and bled viscous pools into the sand, which solidified until they could be lifted in round crusts and cracked with hammers. The children, I remember, took great pains to collect these spillages whole and set them as ornaments in their small and barren gardens, pretending them to be either precious minerals or the lava outflow of a lost volcano.

During that first visit the houses and tower had remained

empty. Corrugated barracks had been built and we were transported daily to and from Lincoln, twenty miles away. The conditions that winter were bad. The foundations continually filled with the rain and snow, causing large areas of concrete to be destroyed and relaid.

Ordinarily, the siting of such a small battery – in this case four guns – would not require such lengthy preparation, but because of the nature of the site, the platform would have remained unstable, requiring constant maintenance or even relocation. Elsewhere, perhaps, that would not have been a problem, but at Cable Point space was at a premium. Accordingly, it was decided that a permanent, reinforced base should be laid and that equally permanent living quarters be built. In addition to these a line of Nissen huts was erected beside the houses along the coast road to the north. The construction of the site was my first real responsibility as a military engineer. The problem, unfortunately, was not only one of engineering, but of accessibility: Cable Point was reached by a narrow road in poor condition, unsuitable for constant use by heavy vehicles. To compound the problem the road ended alongside the houses, over a hundred yards from the lighthouse and the proposed site of the battery.

The major difficulty arose with the initial fixing and filling of the foundations for the gun platform at the head of a sloping beach, which banked steeply and became deceptively saturated at high tide. Our routine, therefore, was dictated by the sea, and a great deal of time was lost or wasted when the opportunity to work and the arrival of the necessary building materials did not coincide. Perhaps also my frustration was aggravated by my desire to be overseas: I was twenty-five and anxious to flex the muscle of my recently acquired commission. The construction of relatively lightweight fortifications on unstable sites was to become my speciality.

During the latter half of December it seemed likely that the work on the site might be abandoned, that the hours of travelling endlessly through the featureless and freezing Lincolnshire countryside would have been wasted, and that my first real task would be a failure. Walking alone along the line of high dunes I cursed the place, and I cursed the men who worked under me.

In January a barrage balloon arrived and work was diverted to lay the foundations for its winch and recovery equipment. Its heavy metal cables were unwound across adjoining fields, slicing suddenly and dangerously upwards as the balloon rose for the first time, announcing our presence to everyone within a radius of thirty miles.

On dark afternoons the small convoys of unprotected shipping would sail silently past and we would stop to watch them, wishing them luck and waving uselessly. They were our only reminder of the war in which the rest of the world was embroiled. Similarly, we stopped work to shout and wave at the coastal patrol aircraft, the Hudsons and heavy-bellied Sunderlands riding like albatrosses over the waves, low enough and near enough for us to see the shape of a head or the flash of yellow.

I left the Light to inspect the now abandoned emplacement, noting with satisfaction where the foundations had withstood three and a half years of battering by the waves. In other places, rusted frameworks protruded and the concrete crumbled, spilling white into the sand of the dunes.

She sat where the line of shingle banked to the sea, and wore a red dress, beneath which she might have been naked. Her knees were drawn up to her chin, her arms folded around them. She dug her feet into the warm pebbles and watched as they rolled from beneath her. It was only as I approached her that I saw the countless places in which the dress had been patched and mended, and the pale circles where the colour had been bleached by the heat, and where the sleeves had been gradually shortened to provide the material for repairs.

She heard me and turned, shielding her eyes and looking up. Having identified me, she turned away, casually throwing individual pebbles into the water. The incoming waves broke in gentle, effortless lines, scarcely breaking the surface before falling away. The sky, as usual, remained pale and cloudless.

'Listen,' she said unexpectedly. The sound of my own movement subsided with the sliding pebbles. I listened and heard the sound of water beneath me.

'It's just the water,' I said, 'driving up through the shingle lower down.'

'I know that,' she said angrily, and once again turned away.

Her hair was short and badly cut, torn at the edges. It was the colour of wheat and it, too, had been bleached by the sun. My intrusion seemed to embarrass her and she twisted at the ends which lay on her shoulder.

'You must be Mary,' I said, moving towards her.

'Who told you?' She became defensive.

'I spoke to your father about –'

'My father's in the war, so you couldn't have done!' She spoke quickly and turned to study me, once again shielding her eyes and leaning back into the shingle. 'You were talking to Mister Owen: I saw you.'

'That's right. Donald Owen. I'm sorry, I thought he –'

'My dad's in the war; I told you.' She laughed at my mistake, but it was a forced laugh – the laugh of a child laughing at an adult.

'Yes, I'm sorry.' I tried to decide what she meant. Her angry and defensive tone suggested it was something she felt strongly about. Or perhaps she simply resented my intrusion and was taking a childish pleasure in my ignorance, which gave her the upper hand. Had he been killed? Was that what she meant?

'At night you can hear the sea come right up under the houses, right past when the tide's up.'

That, I knew, was a geological impossibility, but I did not say so.

'You live in the middle of the terrace,' I said.

She nodded and continued throwing pebbles into the calm water.

'Did you live here before the war?'

19

She nodded again, and I took several steps towards her, debating whether or not to sit beside her on the warm ground, anxious in case she misinterpreted my actions and ran back to report me to her mother.

'You can sit down,' she said, smiling to herself, confirming the extent of her control over what I did, over my discomfort. I sat beside her and drew up my legs. Her skin was heavily tanned and she smelled strongly of soap. She brushed sand from her legs, gathering her dress into her lap to reveal her knees and thighs. She turned and saw me watching, but said nothing. I smiled, nodded and turned away to inspect the horizon for signs of shipping.

'You've come to build the new lifeboat station,' she said.

'Well, I'm here to see about getting rid of the old buildings and foundations. I doubt if I shall have anything to do with the building of the new station.'

'That's what I meant!'

'Yes, well, you were right then, weren't you.'

She detected my irritation, and for a moment I thought she might stand up and leave. Instead, she pulled her dress over her knees, smoothed it down her shins, and smiled. I smiled back and then laughed at the easy and deliberate manner in which she had provoked me.

'You can't really hear the sea under the houses,' she said, confirming her victory and beginning to laugh with me. She pointed to where an exposed pipe ran from the dunes and dribbled dirty water onto the sand. 'Drains.'

I nodded, and from then on we understood each other.

'My mother says you ought to do something about patching up the houses that are already here instead of building new ones for the boat.'

'Oh? They look pretty solid to me.'

She laughed. 'They are, but she always says things like that. She goes on about it all the time. Been going on about it ever since we got back.'

'And have you been back long?'

'They brought us back two years since. There was still a

war, but the man in Lincoln said there was no danger or anything like that. The place we were staying at wasn't much better so it didn't make much difference.' She shrugged.

'You don't like living at Cable Point?' It was a guess rather than a question.

She picked up another handful of shingle and shrugged again. She seemed resigned to the fact, as though there was no possibility of her doing anything about it. As she threw the pebbles I saw the outline beneath her dress, the white of her breasts and underarms.

'I don't mind,' she said after a long pause.

'A bit lonely, I suppose. No one else your own age.' I had seen the other children, but they all seemed to be much younger, embarrassing or unwanted company for a girl her age. Again she shrugged, uncertain of how she felt. Above us, the gulls flew in slow, wide circles, occasionally splashing into the water.

'I've been here before,' I said, sensing the need to change the subject.

'When? I haven't seen you.'

'I came during the war, after you'd all been evacuated, to build the foundations for the guns.'

She nodded, but remained uninterested, expecting a more exciting explanation.

'Were you in the war?'

'No, not really. I never fought, if that's what you mean.'

She relaxed, and repeated proudly what she had already told me about her father. Again her use of the present tense confused me, made me cautious.

'Yes, you said.' My words seemed to hurt her. It occurred to me then that her mother might have used the expression 'in the war' to hide the fact that her father was dead or that, a year later, he still remained posted as missing.

'Whereabouts in the war?'

'Not now! He's not in the war now. The war's finished.'

'I know,' I said impatiently, suspicious of another trick. 'We won.' Through my impatience rose the unexpected memory of three close friends killed by a rogue mine as they dismantled a harbour on the Normandy beaches.

'It finished last year,' she said quietly. 'Last summer.'

'Yes, Mary.'

We both stared out over the sea, at the indistinct patch of smoke above a solitary unseen ship.

'August,' she said.

'Your father was in the Far East, then?' Now I felt guilty, as though I was drawing something from her she did not want to release.

'He's coming home soon, in a few weeks.'

I was uncertain of whether or not she had heard my question. 'That'll be nice for you.' It sounded trite, cold.

She turned to look at me. 'Have you ever heard of a place called Singapore?'

'Your father was there?'

She nodded once and turned back to the sea. 'He was at first, and then they took him to an island somewhere else.'

Above us the gulls began to rise and fall, screaming as they fought over food.

'Have you ever been to Singapore?'

'No, never.'

She turned away, disappointed. 'We thought he was dead,' she said unexpectedly, and stood up, waiting for me to join her.

The following day, as I left the lighthouse, Mary's small brother ran from where he had been standing beside the door to where she sat on one of the empty drums. He stood between her legs and turned to face me. She held his shoulders and pressed her face close to his, whispering. I followed him, uncertain of why he had been so frightened by my appearance or how he would react to my approach.

'No need to run off,' I said. 'You're perfectly welcome to come into the lighthouse as long as you don't tamper with any of the instruments or plans.' I spoke to her rather than the child, smiling at them both to convince them of what I said. The boy looked up at her, waiting for her nod of confirmation. He pointed to me, pushing his other hand into his mouth.

'He's not frightened of going into the Light,' she said.

'What, then? Me? Is he frightened of me?'

She watched me without answering, as though knowing the reason but being uncertain of whether or not to tell me. I crouched down. He pressed himself closer to her, holding her leg. I held out my palms to reassure him, but he was genuinely frightened, his dirty face trembling. She cradled his head and began once again to whisper to him. He looked at her and then back to me, tilting his head and studying me closely. I guessed him to have been five or six, ten years younger than Mary. I smiled but he did not respond.

'It's a wonder to me how you all manage to find things to do all day.'

'We manage,' she said simply. Below her the small boy nodded.

'And today?'

'We were just watching you, that's all.'

I laughed. 'I don't think you're likely to find that very exciting.'

On the site, the men had collected to eat their lunch in the coolness of one of the few remaining buildings. I heard them as they played cards, shouting and laughing at each other.

'We watch the men mostly,' she said, half turning to the source of the noise. The boy turned to her and spoke. 'He wants to know if there are any bombs or bullets or things like that.'

'On the site, you mean?'

'Yes.'

I laughed. 'I should hope not – not with all the hammering and drilling that's going on. I don't think we'd be doing all this if we thought there was any live ammunition still lying around.'

'It was only what he asked,' she said. The small boy began

nodding vigorously. 'But there were guns.' Now her own disappointment became obvious.

'Yes, during the war. But they –'

'We saw them!' she said quickly. 'They were still here when we came back.'

'Yes, I daresay they were.'

'But they never fired.'

The small boy continued nodding and I wondered how much of what we were saying he really understood. He left us to stalk a butterfly which fanned its wings on a block of warm concrete. He lifted his foot over it but Mary tugged at his arm and he walked away.

Several of the men left their shelter and walked to where a makeshift latrine had been dug below ground level. She turned, watching them descend until only their heads were visible. The sound of their splashing embarrassed me, but she seemed unconcerned.

'He's not frightened of the Light,' she said, nodding towards where the small boy watched the men.

'No, you said.'

She hesitated, again about to tell me something, but drawing back. It was because of this, of what she still wanted to tell me, that she had repeated what she had already told me about the boy and the lighthouse.

'It's something different.'

'What, me?'

She nodded.

'Why?'

She waited until the boy had once again joined us, wrapping her arms around his chest before speaking. 'He thought you were our dad.'

'He thought – !'

They waited expressionless. The boy began to nod.

'But why? How?'

'On account of the letters. She told us that he was coming home.'

'And then I arrived?'

She nodded.

'But surely he can't . . . He must know.'

'He's only six.' The small boy nodded and repeated the word 'six'.

'He was only a baby, see, when my dad went off.'

'Yes, I suppose so.'

'He can't remember him, see.' Behind us the last of the men rose out of the ground and she turned to watch. The boy continued to stare at me. I smiled back, trying to imagine his confusion, what my presence might still have meant to him.

'He was watching you in the Light. He does it every day.'

'I think you'd be disappointed,' I said to him, frustrated at being unable to express myself in a way he might understand. 'Your dad's been away fighting in the war. All I've ever done is build things to be either blown up or knocked down.' I waved my hand over the broken ground around us. 'Not much compared to all the adventures your real dad will be able to tell you about.'

'There wasn't no fighting at Singapore,' Mary said coldly. 'They all just surrendered.'

'Who told you that?'

She nodded in the direction of the building from which the men were once again beginning to emerge.

'Don't you believe it,' I said angrily. 'They've all been doing exactly what they're doing now for the past five years. I don't suppose you asked if any of them had ever been any-where near Singapore.'

She shook her head, angry, and confused by what she had been told and what she wanted to believe. The small boy watched her, mimicking her actions as though he, too, understood what was happening.

'It was on the films,' she said quietly. 'We saw them on the films.'

I stood up, unsure of what to say, of how my denial might compare with the propaganda newsreels she so obviously believed. I, too, had seen the film of the official surrender: eighty thousand impeccably emotionless faces, the hopeless eyes, black-ringed and defeated with false, desperate smiles, every one of them uncertain of their future.

'I really think you ought to wait and listen to what your father has to say before you believe everything this lot might tell you.'

She looked at me and then down at her brother. 'It was only him – only him who thought you was our real dad. I never thought it; I knew you weren't. It was only him.' I saw her fist form and press into the boy's arm.

I left them, and as I walked away I heard him cry out in pain. I turned and saw them running towards the houses, Mary still holding his hand, dragging him as he half stumbled and half ran to keep up with her.

two

She entered the room and came to stand beside me. I thought she was going to speak, but instead she began to clear away the dishes and the food neither of us had eaten. I lifted my plate and she took it. I started to apologise for not being hungry, but she simply nodded.

I suppose there are as many ways of grief exhibiting itself as there are people to suffer it. Hers involves moving through the same comforting daily routine of cooking and cleaning in the desperate hope that she will resurface and come to terms with what has happened.

I watched her without letting her know: each time she stopped or sat down she began silently to tremble. I waited for more tears, but none came. In some ways, I wish she would cry. At least then I would be able to comfort her. Instead, her tension and the awaited moment of its breaking have filled the house with an air of awkward and uncomfortable expectancy.

Because my own means of dealing with Michael's death do not correspond with hers we have grown even further apart, and now his absence rather than his presence is the wall between us. Only her feelings of remorse and mine of guilt might draw us back together. But I doubt even this: we have been too long apart. Perhaps if I was able to show my own grief publicly then the situation might be eased; perhaps then

27

it might be easier for her to bear her own. But I cannot, and lying or pretending will only destroy the few fragile ties we are able to maintain now that we are alone.

I listened to her as she moved around the kitchen, to the rattle of crockery, the sound of running water, and I cursed the military procedures and distance which separated us from our son's body and hoped that the funeral service would prove to be the release it is designed to be.

She returned carrying two cups. 'Coffee,' she said, putting them into saucers already on the table and sitting opposite me. The china rattled, registering and then exaggerating her nervousness. She lifted her hand and studied it, each finger, each ring, as though expecting to see something she had never before seen. I held her wrist and stopped the movements. She began to move her free hand towards me, looked up, and then withdrew them both – as if unsure of what her actions might suggest, as if she was making an unwilling contact, however slight, the significance of which she did not understand.

Perhaps I should have been stronger and forced her out of her grief; perhaps that is what she wanted me to do but did not know how to ask. I withdrew my own hands and began to drink. She watched me. When I looked up she turned away.

The muted sounds of traffic filtered into the room, and the open french windows let in the morning heat and a rectangle of brilliant sunlight which lay across the polished floor. Cane furniture stood on the lawn, but neither of us used it. An unopened paper lay on the grass beside one of the chairs, stained with cuttings and the morning dew. A bee hung in the open doorway and the tips of climbing roses made curling, investigative gestures into the room.

She closed her hand around her cup, causing faint elliptical ripples over its surface. She stared at the moving pattern as though something was being drawn out of her, as though when the ripples stopped her grief would be gone.

*

As we prepared to lay the foundations for one of the larger buildings, a slab of already solid concrete shifted, overturning a platform on which three men were working. Two managed to jump clear, but the third was forced by the collapsing platform into a trench. He was unhurt, only the heavy plank upon which he had been standing preventing him from climbing out. He sat in a shallow pool of water and swore. The men above him began to make fun of him. Others ran to join them. They were still laughing as they began to lever the plank from above him and as the unsettled slab of concrete slid into the trench and crushed his legs. He screamed only once and then became unconscious. Around us, a flock of hidden gulls rose from the workings, flapping vigorously to get airborne, the sound of their exertions filling the air.

I administered morphine, and the bleeding stopped of its own accord. Later, we were able to lift him out of the trench and carry him to the road. I sat beside him for the remainder of the day, waiting for the lorries and watching his face, anxious in case he regained consciousness and I was unable to help him. The birds resettled, strutting over the open ground around us. As they came close I threw stones and clapped them away. I learned later that both the man's legs had been amputated.

It was hearing of Michael's injuries that revived the memory of the accident. I had cared for and visited the man, but I had not been to see my own son. I had even written a detailed report on the circumstances of the accident, suggesting half a dozen reasons why it might have occurred.

When I saw him afterwards he thanked me and made a forced joke about the loose flaps of his pyjama legs. He told me that the nurses had sewn the bottoms together, but that they would not cut off the material, insisting each day on rolling them out for him to see. He began to cry, reaching out to soothe the pains which pulled his non-existent muscles taut. Afterwards, he asked about the others still working on the site. He asked me to thank them for what they had tried to do for him. We spoke of his wife and of the war. She lived in Bir-

mingham and had been unable to visit him. He made excuses
for her. I agreed with him and told him whatever he wanted to
hear.

That was the last time I saw him. The trench was filled in
and a new one excavated.

Perhaps if I had been with her to visit Michael his death
might have been easier to bear. It is little consolation, but
perhaps sharing that experience might have been some comfort to her. All I could think of when the news of his injuries
reached us was of the man in the trench, the laughter, his
scream, and the gulls rising around us like torn paper in a
wind.

I imagined Michael at home, overcoming what had happened. I imagined us together, telling him about the man.
When he died, I was caught off balance, knowing neither what
to believe nor how to behave. It is this which she mistakes for
callousness, for not caring.

She wore the same red and faded dress and stood beside the
lighthouse door, one leg bent against the white wall.

Behind me, the men gathered beside the road. I nodded to
the women who stood in their doorways and watched the
smaller children as they chased each other through the clouds
of dust thrown up by the departing lorries, encouraged by the
men who shouted to them and applauded their efforts.

Cones of sand and rubble lined the road. Beyond them
stretched the broken foundations, outlines staked in wood and
rope, machinery and tools draped with tarpaulins.

'My mother's sent this.' She pointed to a lantern at her feet
and rubbed at the smudges of soot across her palms.

'Paraffin?'

She nodded. 'We have electric in the houses.' She stood
back to look up the curving wall behind us. 'Do you live in
it all?'

'No. I've been given the ground floor to – '

'Why don't you go off with the rest of them every day?
Are you their boss?' She spoke quietly, as though the questions

had been prepared. When I answered she tried to appear un-interested, clapping her hands to the whitewash and picking at the flakes which came away.

'Yes, I suppose I am their boss. And as for not going back to Lincoln each night, well . . .'

'My dad used to be a coastguard.'

'Yes, I know.'

'Used to be four of them. Mister Owen was the boss. The others went off, but Mister Owen stayed with us. My mother says that when they build the new station he won't be the boss any more – she says they'll be bringing someone new in.' She stopped, waiting for me to either deny or confirm her guesses. When I simply nodded she turned away disappointed.

I moved towards the door and she followed, holding the frame and peering into the dark interior.

'Come in, please.'

She led the way inside.

'I could clean it up for you.' The offer surprised me. I explained that in refurbishing the tower the builders were likely to make a considerably greater mess.

'No, not for them – for you. For now. Dusting and stuff like that.'

'Have a look round if you like.'

'No need. We used to come in here all the time before the war. Mister Christie used to let us go up to the top room. It's empty now, but there used to be a ladder that went up through the ceiling to where they kept the Light.' She seated herself in the room's only comfortable chair, her legs hanging above the floor. 'This is Mister Christie's chair.'

'Well, I'm sure he won't mind me using it for a while.'

'Is he coming back?'

'I don't know. I don't even know where he went.'

But she wasn't listening. Instead she began to inspect my additions to the room.

'What do you eat?'

'Eat?'

'My mother says she'll cook for you if you let her have some coupons.'

'I'm sorry, I haven't any.'

She seemed disappointed and fell back into her seat, raising her legs and holding them together.

'Tea?' I asked.

'I'd rather have coffee.'

'When did you last have any of that?'

'I've never had any. I just wanted to try it.'

I searched the cartons of food with which I had been provided and took out a small tin embossed with the word Coffee. 'Here. A present.'

She took it and traced her fingers over the raised lettering. 'This can be payment,' she said.

'Payment?'

'For doing your cleaning.'

I realised that once again I had been outmanoeuvred.

'I can come in tomorrow morning while you're out at work.'

I nodded and continued to prepare the tea.

Despite the heat outside, the interior of the lighthouse remained consistently cool. A strip of sunlight fell in from the open door and another lay across the wide sill of the single small window.

She drank her tea and pulled a face. 'No sugar?'

I laughed again. 'When did you last have sugar to waste in tea?'

'I don't usually drink tea.' She put the cup on the floor and drew her legs into the chair.

There was the same strong smell of soap I had noticed at our first meeting. She saw me watching and pulled the neckline of her dress towards me.

'It's soap. You can smell it if you want.'

I said there was no need, and that it was a pleasant smell, better than cement.

'She washes it all the time.' She smelled the cloth and pulled a face.

'Haven't you any others?' I regretted asking before I had finished speaking.

'Course I have!' She smoothed the material down over her chest and stomach. 'Mister Christie used to have a round cupboard that fitted against that wall,' she said, and turned to point to where the vague outline still remained. 'He made it himself. We saw him do it. He must have taken it with him.'

After that she became quiet, the silence of the room broken only by the knot of flies which circled the ceiling. After a few minutes she looked up, watching me closely and rolling the small tin across her legs. The distant sound of the other children made us both turn. She listened and then turned back to me.

'We filled the lamp before I brought it.'

'What? Oh, yes, the lamp.'

She left the chair and stood beside me, demonstrating how the wick worked. The explanation was unnecessary, but I listened and nodded and repeated what she said.

'I was only ten when he went off,' she said unexpectedly, her face beside mine, the smell of soap stronger than ever. She paused, as though the simple revelation was of some significance to us both.

'It'll be nice for him to see you all again.' It sounded insincere and cold, but something in the way she spoke of her father made me uneasy, gave me the impression that to suggest anything else would have been to intrude upon something she was unwilling to share.

'We had a book with pictures of a desert island in it.' Now she spoke excitedly, leaning across the table towards me. 'Palm trees with coconuts and all these animals. Some men had funny boats and there was a volcano with smoke.' She paused. 'He was on an island like that.' Then she stopped, studying my face for confirmation that I believed her.

'Yes, I'm sure he was,' I said.

'We saw pictures when we were moved away, evacuated. Proper pictures in a Picture House where we were staying. And afterwards Mister Christie said – ' She hesitated and

33

lifted her hands from the table. 'Do you think all desert islands are the same?'

'Mostly,' I said.

'But they don't all have volcanoes?'

'No, I shouldn't think so.'

'Or wild animals.'

'No.'

She shook her head, finally unconvinced by the fantasies she had woven around her missing father.

'We had a letter.'

'When? Today?'

She looked up at me, surprised, and I realised that it was probably the same letter she had mentioned during our first meeting.

'Before that we used to get others just saying where he was – no writing from him or anything. They used to come from London. At Christmas she used to put them all up like they were cards or something.'

I nodded and she looked once again to the open doorway.

three

After a morning alone, I walked into the garden, feeling the warm stone of the path and blinded by the sun as it was reflected off a pane of glass in a brilliant copper square. There was a faint smell of petról and the ever-present hum of traffic.

Tomorrow his body will be flown home and the following day he will be buried. These two facts dominate everything I think or want to say. Several of his friends have written to us asking permission to attend the funeral. There were even letters of condolence from some of those who were serving with him. I thought that the sight of uniforms at the ceremony might upset her, but she read the letters and said that she would not mind if they attended. I doubt if they will be given permission or leave to come. I suspect also that she is uncertain of her own feelings, and that the effect will be greater than she anticipates. One man has written to explain that he had been with Michael when the explosion had occurred, and that he would be unable to make the trip because of his own injuries. With the letter was a blurred Instamatic photograph of himself and Michael taken only two days previously. There was writing on the back which he had scribbled out – something obscene perhaps. They were both smiling exaggerated, confident smiles, their arms around each other's shoulders and holding glasses of beer towards the camera.

She had taken the picture, pointing out to me the features

of his face, commenting on vague family likenesses, on the way he held his mouth when he smiled, on the way his eyes flicked away from the camera. She pointed these things out as though I had been previously unaware of them, as though I did not know they were our son. But I did not argue, and she in turn began to remember other occasions, other photographs.

I left the path and stood in the centre of the lawn. A cat basked on the high wall which separated the garden from the street, turning casually to watch me, ready to jump down and run. It stared at me, challenging me to enter into some kind of silent contest.

I closed my eyes and tried to fix my son. I saw him in uniform, posing beside his mother and then myself during his last leave. I saw him as a young teenager and then as a small boy, crying before his second day at grammar school, the long arm of his blazer held stiffly from his side, the leather satchel which creaked as he walked. Then I made the mistake of trying to imagine him as he had been in the hospital.

My eyes remained closed, but all I could see was the man in the narrow trench, screaming, the slab across his legs.

I opened my eyes. The cat was gone, and as I turned, an upstairs curtain fell slowly back into place.

During that first winter there were only two airfields between Cable Point and Lincoln, both of which were being extended in preparation for the arrival, the following year, of the American squadrons to be based there.

By 1946 and the occasion of my second visit, two new bases had been built, both of them considerably larger than the earlier ones, and both still lined with the streamlined silver bombers which had seemed so ahead of their time. The fuselages of the aircraft were decorated with good luck charms and strange-sounding names which added to their brash Americanness. Names such as Bucking Bronco, Jersey Jets and Candy Girl. There were horses and women, cartoon characters, and the badges and emblems of the cities and states from which the aircrew came.

Billeted on that first occasion in Lincoln, I shared quarters with several of the engineers working on the runway extensions. They spoke enthusiastically of their work, of the new techniques being employed for the first time. I became anxious in case I, too, was assigned to work on the fields. For that reason, I began once again to despair at the slow progress being made at Cable Point, at the delays and each new problem. I despaired at the overpowering grey skies, at the feeling of absolute exposure, and at our helplessness in the face of the biting winds which tore in from the North Sea to shower us with rain and hail, and which each night froze the water in the workings.

In the year since the war had ended, the new bases had deteriorated rapidly with disuse. Those which had been abandoned were cut into geometric patterns by the grass and yellow weeds which forced themselves up through the concrete joints, and by the mosses which exploited damp walls and shadowed interiors. At some of the bases, service and administrative crews remained for up to three years, awaiting transfer home, their enthusiasm drained and growing resentful at being forgotten, suddenly unwanted strangers in that alien landscape.

USAAF Walsham was the nearest of the bases to Cable Point, six miles inland. Prior to its construction, the RAF had used the coast as a collecting point, strings of aircraft moving in wide circles as their flying formations were established or as smaller groups joined together. We would watch them circling like buzzards as we awaited our transport back to barracks. When we could not see them, we listened for the droning of their unsynchronised engines, guessing at their targets.

In the home of one of the former coastguards hung a heavy leather flying jacket, lined with cream sheepskin and badly torn on one sleeve. The man boasted of having exchanged it for a crate of fish less than a week after VE day. I saw him wearing the jacket as he watched us at work amongst the rubble. He offered to sell it to me, and when I refused he insisted that he would never part with it. He offered it to several of the men. They also refused, and despite the persistent heat, he continued to wear the jacket and extol its virtues.

On the airfields the discarded silver aircraft stood in broken lines, their painted symbols flaking, sagging lopsidedly on deflated tyres. A few were maintained but most awaited being broken up. There was no urgency, and once abandoned their own rate of deterioration, like the bases', was remarkably fast. Parts were salvaged to maintain the serviceable aircraft, and when one of these flew every member of the remaining ground staff would watch, tensing against the expectation of an unsuccessful take-off or landing. Salvage crews roamed from base to base to retrieve necessary parts, leaving the long silver bodies hollow, broken and open to the rain. Whole engines, even wings, were dismantled and transported through the narrow country lanes.

At the beginning of that summer there had been an accident, seen from both Lincoln and Cable Point, when the tailplane of a bomber had shaken free and the aircraft had spun earthwards in a contorted spiral, its agony prolonged by the four engines which continued to pull and push at the falling body. It had been a warm day, and those who witnessed the crash commented on the way in which the sun flashed on the silver fuselage as it fell, heliographing its final, useless call for help. Four aircrew and nine others were killed in the explosion. Afterwards, each time one of the planes circled the coast, the men and women at Cable Point would leave their homes to stand and watch, tracing the white lines and pointing to the rippling cross of shadow as it moved over the fields ahead of them. The children, too, left their games to fire imaginary guns into the air.

I saw them once, five of them including Mary, hidden in the dunes, crowding together in the loose sand as one of the aircraft passed overhead. They pointed to it with both hands, ten arms following the streaming wake. One of the boys shouted 'Crash!' and the others joined in the chant, rising to a crescendo as the plane passed directly above them, and as they felt the shock of its shadow. Their voices subsided and they began to laugh. Only Mary stood to watch as the aircraft continued inland. I crouched down to avoid being seen. She continued to point until the silver shape was no longer visible. After that she slid down the dunes to join the others, speaking to them and causing them to become instantly silent, only her young brother still throwing up handfuls of sand and watching as it covered his feet.

One of the older boys crawled to the rim of the depression in which they sat. He crossed his legs, buried his hands and continued to search the sky, watching the gulls and lowering his gaze to the distant horizon of the sea.

Mary lifted her brother to the inland-facing slope and held him above the ground as he urinated, staining the pale sand in a growing circle. In her arms he appeared much younger than he was, a baby almost. She spoke to him and he laughed. She began to swing him and he shouted for more. She began slowly, but as her movements became more and more violent she began to sink into the sand, his flailing legs hitting her back. The small boy hovered on the brink of excitement and fear. Then he began to cry, shouting for her to stop. The others watched, none of them daring to intervene. She continued to swing him, buried now to her knees. The boy stopped screaming and she slowed her movements, letting him fall. He stood, but fell again as his balance returned. She continued to spin, holding out her arms, her red dress rising in a plate above her knees. The small boy retrieved his shorts and ran, still half-naked, to where the others waited.

The boy on the crest of the dune shouted to them and pointed skywards. I looked up and saw a second pinpoint of reflected light and the white thread drawn out behind it. Again they pointed and began to chant. The aircraft turned in a gentle curve towards the coast and they ran to the opposite side of the dune, bent double, as though even from that great height they might still be seen.

In the silence which followed, I heard only the sawing noise of the drills and the drumming of the pneumatic hammers as they probed and created weaknesses in the exposed foundations; I heard the gulls and the voices of individual men. I waited, watching, unable to stand upright without being seen by the children. Mary led the chanting and then fell silent as the others took it up, louder than before, and with stabbing motions of their outstretched arms. She watched them, and then she left them, climbing out of the dunes in the direction of the houses. Only her brother ran after her.

I stood and followed them, passing the children in the hollow, who by now had stopped chanting, occupying themselves instead by throwing sand at each other and putting on a show of childishness as children do to hide themselves. I waved to them and threw down a coil of rope I had salvaged from the site of the balloon. They fought each other in the struggle to retrieve it and claim it as their own.

Mary crossed the whitewashed end of the terrace and walked towards the working men. Seeing her, they began to shout. She waved to them and shouted some of their names. They waved back and shared private jokes about her. One of them offered her a cigarette. She took it and held it in her mouth as he lit it. Then she spat it out, laughing at the man's curses as he searched for the wasted tobacco. The others laughed and applauded her. She climbed onto a concrete pillar and stood above them. She curtsied, bending forward and then standing upright, the edges of her dress still held at arms' length. I saw the outline of her legs and heard as their applause died. Climbing down from her pedestal, she ran into the small garden of her home. She saw me and stopped, looking from me to her brother. I asked her what she had been doing. She lied and said that she was helping her mother. Then she said it was none of my business what she did. From the open doorway came the sound of her mother's voice, singing. She pointed up to where the lines of vapour faded behind the invisible plane.

'It's going to Walsham,' she said.

I doubted it: the lines continued too far inland. 'Probably.'

'No! It is!' she insisted.

I turned to look, but was in no mood to agree with her simply to placate her. 'Is it?' I said. 'So what?' But when I turned for her response, the garden was empty and she was inside, singing with her mother, her voice a high, mocking tone. I looked in and saw their outlines against the light of a rear window.

Behind me the drilling resumed, filling the air with cones of blue smoke which rippled in the heat. Some of the men stood and watched me, either nodding or turning away ashamed as I approached. They wore folded handkerchiefs over their mouths, tanned and naked to the waist and running with sweat. Their heads, backs and arms were coated in a fine powder which, from a distance, gave them a curious, statue-like appearance as they rested amongst the broken buildings and piles of rubble.

As had become their custom, the women of Cable Point gathered to watch the lorries as they prepared to leave, their less demonstrative – probably resentful – husbands remaining indoors.

Of the line of six houses, only five were occupied, the sixth being considered unsafe following the collapse of an upstairs floor during the four years in which the houses had been abandoned. Of those remaining, one was inhabited solely by Donald Owen, whom I had mistaken for Mary's father.

The husband of another woman had been drowned in the North Atlantic. A neighbour informed me that he had been in the Merchant Navy and that his ship had been torpedoed. She had spoken in a low voice, wanting to tell me more, but clearly anxious that she should not have been identified as the source of the information. That privilege, I realised, belonged to the widow alone.

The men preferred to wait until the lorries had gone before venturing outdoors, emerging together to inspect the demolition work, to salvage whatever might be available, and to smoke and make guesses at where the new station was to be built. They sat amongst the debris like the survivors of a great disaster, staring back at their wives and homes. They resented our presence and the changes we were forcing upon them – changes which signalled the end of their own livelihoods at Cable Point. I knew from consultation with the architects responsible for the new station that none of them would be given positions of any importance at the new station, and that a line of more substantial housing was being planned alongside that already existing. There had even been talk of demolishing the exposed terrace. But the men knew nothing of this as they dragged at buried timbers, shouting to the women and swearing in the afternoon heat in a poor echo of those already departed.

Along with the rebuilding, the lighthouse was also to be refurbished and a new light installed. It would later be necessary to tear out the collar of leaded glass to allow the installation of a reinforced cradle in which the new light would sit. A new keeper was to be appointed, and the men among the ruins speculated without any real hope on their own chances of securing the job, each encouraging the others with his own guarded flattery and expectations.

The women shouted, calling them names and laughing at their efforts. But the men refused to be drawn, angry, perhaps, at the comparisons frequently made between them and the younger men who came and went with the lorries.

During the long summer evenings, the women would bring out chairs, sitting together beside their open doors, holding repeated conversations and turning constantly to face the setting sun as it fell towards the level horizon ahead of them. The children ran around them, the younger ones falling asleep in their mothers' arms or on the warm paths at their feet.

A troop of semi-feral cats inhabited the disused buildings, and they, too, emerged each evening to scavenge over the deserted site, tempted by the food left by the men. Some of the animals moved equally confidently in and out of the houses; others shied away from even the slightest contact, racing silently away from the stones thrown at them by the men and children.

The door of the lighthouse was often open, and when they discussed me the women lowered their voices. I watched them from the shadowed interior, saw their turned heads and pointing arms. But I heard nothing of what they said, and it would have been considered unfriendly of me to remain apart from them, to deprive them of the novelty of my presence. And so I sat with them, answering their questions about who I was, where I came from and what I was there to do. The men were interested in the workings; the women in me.

On one such evening I left the lighthouse later than usual, just as the lower edge of the sun touched the ground. Mary and her mother were alone, sitting against the wall on either side of the doorway, rubbing their arms as the last of the day's heat was lost to the clear sky and cold night. I heard the cats and saw two of the men walking over the foundations away from me.

Mary saw me first and shouted. Her mother looked up, instinctively smoothing the creases from her stained apron. I knew her to be about thirty-five or six, but she looked older, traces of her former good looks remaining in her eyes and lips.

'I'm sorry, I didn't mean to disturb you.'

'No, no. Nonsense.' She smiled nervously, not knowing what else to say.

Mary stared directly at me, turning away only as I nodded to her. She rose from her seat and stood against the wall, looking from me to her mother. She seemed uneasy, as though she would rather have been indoors, listening to our conversation without being seen or involved.

'We were just catching the last of the warmth.'

'Yes, I see. I'm afraid I was rather busy tonight, and before I knew it – ' I shrugged, nodding at the broken outline of the sun.

'Come and sit down.'

'No, thank you. I won't stop. To tell you the truth, I've been sitting all day and I've come out to stretch my legs.' I arched my back to suggest stiffness. She smiled and nodded, relieved, I suspect, that I would not stay. Mary returned to her seat, as though a crisis had passed and she was now willing to remain with us. There was a further awkward silence, during which I turned to watch the two men. Mary whispered something, and sat back, her arms folded.

'I don't know what they find to do out there every night,' the woman said. 'Perhaps they're out looking for any treasure you might have turned up.' She laughed. I joined her, telling her they were welcome to whatever they wanted from the site. Mary watched us both, embarrassed by her mother's laughter. In the gardens of the other houses lay the coils of rusted cable and sheets of corrugated iron already retrieved.

'Mary tells me her father's coming home,' I said.

The woman looked immediately anxious, raising her hand to her mouth in yet another instinctive, nervous gesture.

'Yes. In a few weeks, we expect. He's been out in the Far East, Singapore . . .'

'Yes, Mary explained.'

She turned to her daughter. Mary looked up at me and narrowed her eyes – whether in anger or as a warning, I wasn't sure. Turning to her mother, she shook her head and reached out to hold her hand.

'Four years,' the woman said, looking down to avoid my eyes.

Watching her, I regretted having raised the subject. I felt angry and ashamed, conscious also of the fact that we were both being in some way manipulated by the girl who sat and watched us.

'You see, he's been . . . We didn't . . .'

'I think I understand,' I said, uncertain of whether she did not want to tell me in front of her daughter or simply because of her own uncertainties about what had happened to him, about what to expect. There was, I realised, a considerable difference between the expectations of the man's daughter and the realities to be faced by his wife.

'Yes, four years. It's a long time.' She smiled as she spoke, folding her palms into her lap.

44

'He'll notice some changes,' I said, waving my hand over the demolished buildings, unsure of her feelings and of how to change the subject. I wondered if she spoke to the other women about him.

'Singapore,' Mary suddenly announced.

The woman turned and smiled, reaching to hold her daughter's knee. There seemed something inexplicably and hopelessly pathetic in the woman's uncertainty compared to the conviction of her daughter and the way in which *she* had spoken to me about her father.

'That's right,' the woman said. 'Singapore.' She said it as though praising a clever child who had learned a simple fact.

'Singapore,' Mary repeated, staring hard at her mother's face, at once comforting her and challenging her to respond.

'We're going to have a new wireless set,' Mary said as the woman was about to speak. 'We can listen to it with him when he gets home.' The simplicity of her words and the childishness in her voice seemed false, somehow forced for her mother's benefit.

'Yes, I'm sure you will,' I said, hoping to let her know by the tone of my voice that I understood what she was doing.

The woman nodded. She seemed lost, content simply to agree with her daughter and to be reassured by her, to follow in her confident wake.

'And we won't live here, either, because once he gets a new job then we're going to move away.' Again the same forced childish arrogance and certainty.

The woman looked surprised, as though hearing the suggestion for the first time. But she, too, began to smile and nod her head, as though preferring to believe her daughter's expectations rather than her own.

'Do you know exactly when he's arriving, when he's landing? Have they given you a – '

'Landing?' She turned to face me, pulling her hand from her daughter's leg. 'Landing!' She laughed coldly. 'He's not landing; he's been in a hospital down in London for the past two months. All we're waiting for is for him to come up here.' She repeated the word 'landing' as though it was a clever joke. Mary repeated it and they both laughed, touching each other before turning to me and apologising.

I wondered about how the man had spent the last year. Certainly, the laughter of his wife and daughter seemed inexcusably cruel after what he had endured. But perhaps this was their protection against what the woman at least must surely have been expecting.

'We had letters,' she said, adding quickly: 'Oh, not from him, but from the Army, some even from Singapore after the war had finished. They told us where he was and everything: it wasn't as if we didn't know.' Now she seemed to be making excuses for their behaviour.

'You must be excited,' I said, wishing I hadn't, the words hanging between us in a void where no genuine contact had yet been made.

'Excited?' She genuinely did not seem to have considered the prospect.

'Of course we are,' Mary said angrily.

But the woman remained uncertain, confused by what I was suggesting.

I left them and returned to the Light. As I was about to enter, I saw Donald Owen leave the site and cross the road towards them. He entered the small garden and said something to Mary. She went indoors. Then he and the woman stood together and watched me. He held his hand against the wall and pointed to where another man moved noisily over the broken ground. He left her, and she stood alone, watching the man as he dragged a length of timber through the collapsing rubble.

There had been a warning beacon at Cable Point since the middle of the seventeenth century. Since that time, the sea had scraped back the coastline to a distance of almost a mile. Old photographs chronicled the years of most rapid erosion, and on maps the broken lines of former coasts ran like ripples into the sea. The first permanent structure recognisable as a lighthouse was constructed in 1860 and replaced on the same foundations by the present structure thirty years later.

As I prepared to embank the anti-aircraft battery, I received a copy of part of a local history, itself thirty years old, consisting of conflicting accounts written over the previous century. Some of the sources were identified, others remained obscure or guessed at; some were straightforward factual accounts of the building of the Light and houses; other writers embellished these sparse accounts with histories of major storms and shipwrecks – some up to fifty miles away, beyond all sight and sound of the Light.

What interested me was the fact that until twenty years after the construction of the present Light, there had been no permanent road linking Cable Point with the villages further inland. Even now those villages were only visible from the summit of the dunes, identifiable by the cushions of trees which surrounded them. It was, several of the history's contributors noted, easier for contact to be made and for provisions to be brought to Cable Point by sea, using coasters and the small boats still kept at the station, than for overland transport to be used. All the stone and heavy timbers used in the construction of the Light and houses had been landed at a point three miles to the north and carried by horse and cart along the relatively stable spine of the dunes.

Two badly reproduced photographs accompanied the history. In one, six women, barefoot and swathed in heavy shawls and aprons, stood beside a mound of silver bodies. Each held a slender knife, and beside each stood a wicker basket filled with the same empty and shining bodies. Above the figures hung a swarm of scavenging gulls, and behind them rose the white finger of the tower. In the middle distance stood two men, their backs to the camera. The faces of the women were hard and bronzed, Red Indian-like in their strength and lack of emotion. The hands of one of the women were blurred, as though she had continued to gut the fish as the photographer counted out the seconds of their fixing.

The second photograph was of the houses with the Light

behind them. The stone and mortar of the walls was revealed, awaiting the first protective coat of rendering and whitewash. The windows and doors showed as black shadows, and smoke rose from each of the six chimneys. A solitary woman stood in the shadow of one doorway, a naked child with its hand to its face beside her.

I had been given the brief history as a supplement to a letter explaining that the rights of the inhabitants were to be respected, and that as little unnecessary disturbance as possible was to be caused. The word 'unnecessary' amused me. How did they expect a tiny, isolated community like Cable Point not to be disturbed by the daily influx of over sixty men, machinery, and the installation of what amounted to almost five acres of defensive fortifications? I need not have worried: by the time we arrived, the inhabitants had already been evacuated.

Upon my return four years later, I realised that it had been I, and not the enemy, who had brought the war to Cable Point, and I who had kept it there long after the fighting had finished.

On the site plans, only the Light and the terrace of houses were shown as permanent structures. The road was represented as a broken line which petered out where the houses began. It might once have extended a further fifty yards towards the Light, but had long since become covered with sand and soil. Now, the boundary of the road was defined by the women who brushed the sand from it – not because they wanted to keep the road clear, but because they wanted to keep the sand from their homes and desperate gardens. Upon seeing the women for the first time, I realised that some of them might have been descended from the fishwives in the photograph. The colour in their faces had been drawn out, but there was still a hardness, and a suspicion of anyone or anything beyond that with which they were already intimately familiar.

On the upper edge of the map, the featureless line of the beach and dunes had been inscribed with a half circle, half a mile to the north of where the balloon had been sited. At first I guessed it to be the foundations of yet another, earlier fortification (the reinforced bases of some pillboxes would have been circular in design, although the location in the dune line argued against it being such).

One Sunday, alone at the site, I decided to investigate. I walked to the balloon site, now nothing more than a square of crumbling concrete upon which coils of rusted cable lay like giant worm casts. The pale sand with its skirt of shingle stretched northwards in an unbroken line, disappearing into the haze. The sea was again calm, the waves lacking the momentum to do anything but soak into the beach. I continued walking, constantly turning to measure what I thought to be half a mile from where the winch had been. Ahead of me, intermittently hidden by the dunes, I saw the top of a ladder. Set into the ground, and invisible except from directly above, was a perfectly circular stone-lined pit or well, twelve feet deep and approximately twenty in diameter. Over it lay a rusted grille, through which the ladder had been inserted. A scree of sand a yard deep collected around the base of the curving wall.

On the surface of the sand lay sheets of newspaper and empty bottles. Perhaps it was to here that the children came each morning as they trooped single file along the road, up through the brambles and into the dunes.

I inspected the circular wall, surprised by its solidity and the high standard of the masonry. Very likely it had been built as the foundation of an earlier, or even second light. The nature of the construction would date it at around the time of the first permanent tower.

The shadow of the grille crisscrossed every surface, only a slender crescent of sunlight penetrating the upper edge of the well.

I left and returned to the site of the winch. From there the line of the dunes fell and I was able to see the distant houses in the elongated shadow of the Light.

I learned later that a second tower had been planned, and

that what I had found were its foundations. Apparently there had been a competition between two landowners to erect the first light and thus qualify for government levies. My informant was uncertain of the details of the race to build, only that the foundations of the most northerly tower had been abandoned following an accident in which two labourers had been killed. He hinted that sabotage had been the cause, but refused to be drawn any further. I asked him if anyone ever visited the site. He laughed, shook his head, and said that perhaps the children still went there.

After my visit, I returned to the lighthouse and fell asleep in the armchair. I dreamt of the children, of their elaborate processions and rituals, and of a coastline fringed with countless lights, white in the daytime like blunted teeth, but brilliant and flashing through the night. When I awoke it was evening and the round room had grown cold.

four

With my eyes closed, and feeling the warmth on my face, the noise of the traffic beyond the wall fades until it is almost inaudible. And as it dies, so the noise of the insects which surround me rises. Without fully understanding why – perhaps because I could not imagine how he had looked during the months before his death, only his crying and shouting face as a schoolboy and teenager – I said his name. It seemed to echo, my mouth silently forming the word over and over.

I opened my eyes. There was no one to have seen or heard, only his mother who might have been watching as I stood at the centre of the lawn rising from the pool of my shadow as though from a hole in the ground. The birdsong increased, rising and falling above and below common repeated notes. The noise of the traffic returned, and I waited, still motionless, empty and ready and wanting to believe that my own grief had at last risen to the surface.

For the past eighteen months, ever since his first tour of duty in Ireland, we had waited to hear of his injury or death, neither of us admitting our fears to the other, or saying the things any other parent in that same situation might have said. Rather than share and seek comfort in our common fears, we hid them, and, unspoken, they maintained the growing distance between us.

I had watched her tense at each news report, straining for

every detail. And afterwards there would be no relief, only the insistent doubt that a mistake had been made, or that another man's death signalled a resurgence in the violence which would lead to his own. Perhaps preparing ourselves for the news of his death had worked against us; perhaps we had come to regard as inevitable that which, until it happened, remained unlikely or statistically improbable. We had become too accustomed to dealing with false alarms, to not believing. At his insistence we had stopped watching the television news, turning instead to the papers in which the acts of violence and deaths appeared less immediate but more final. The unread paper on the lawn contains the news of his own death. In any case, I argued, we would be informed of any injury long before it was released to the media. But even that was no longer true: they simply announced that an unidentified soldier had been killed, which only increased and prolonged the agony of not knowing.

We had been sent details of how we should correspond with him, of the importance of omitting all unnecessary details from both the letter and envelope. Occasionally we had received military mail intended for him but delivered to us to await his return. The first of these forms had arrived with the impact of a wartime telegram, but eventually they were delivered printed with details of what they contained. I read the envelopes aloud, and we used these false alarms as cause for silent celebration, leaving the papers unread and moving temporarily together in our relief.

She kept photographs of his girlfriends, posing with his arm around their shoulders, kissing them for the camera, their eyes watching him as he waited to release them. In Belfast there had been an Army nurse about whom he had told us a great deal.

This had been his second tour. Londonderry, he assured us, was considerably safer than the border where he had previously been stationed. He had announced the fact publicly, and for her sake I had agreed with him.

I remember the occasion of his very first leave, stepping

from the train, standing in his uniform to be admired, the looks of other passengers, his new moustache adding years to his face and making him look even more like a soldier. I insisted on carrying his bag, lost to my own memories as he and she walked ahead of me to the car. He had put on weight and seemed taller. I drove and he sat beside me. I saw her in the rear-view mirror, watching him closely and smiling. On that first occasion he had spoken excitedly about what he had done, the places he had been, the people he had met. She listened to him, turning away as her eyes caught mine. It was only later, after he had gone, that she began to repeat the things he had told us, asking me if I thought they were true and what they meant.

Perversely, the news of his injury came as a relief: he was injured and not dead: our waiting was over. Accompanying the official notification was a list of the preparations to be made and an outline of the procedure whereby he would be returned home. It was possible, they suggested, that his injuries, regardless of their severity, might not fully disqualify him from a continued career in the Army. There was a pamphlet outlining the terms of his release should he or we so wish it, or should his injuries prove greater or more permanent than expected.

I read the forms aloud, and she had cried. Four days later we were informed of his death.

It is less than two hours since the captain and the padre left, taking with them the last of our uncertainty and hope. Two hours, but already I seem to have known about and understood his death for many years.

Mary and her mother sat together at the entrance to an excavated shelter, whose turf-covered roof had collapsed to carpet the floor. Beside them, the younger children sat in a group, scraping at the crushed and powdered aggregate of the walls, their legs over the rim of a shallow trench.

'Lovely evening,' the woman said, announcing my approach to her daughter. She held a folded newspaper across her lap and seemed more confident and self-assured than at our last meeting. The children turned and Mary's young brother climbed from the trench and ran towards me. He stood with his fingers in his mouth, looking up.

'He's taken a shine to you.'

'Yes, I suppose he has.' I remembered what Mary had told me about the boy mistaking me for his father. I wondered if the woman knew, and wanted to explain, but felt reluctant to do so in case I offended her or revived her anxiety.

She spoke first: 'She told me as how he thought you was his dad.'

Mary moved between us and pulled the child towards her.

'Yes, I'm sorry – '

She interrupted me with a laugh and a wave of her hand. Mary, too, began to laugh, glancing from me to her mother. The woman stopped, saying that she hoped I hadn't been offended. I in turn expressed my own fears that it was she, and not I, who was most likely to have been offended.

'Me? No. He was only a baby, see, when his dad – when he went off.'

'Yes; Mary explained.'

She turned to her daughter with a sudden, worried look. Mary watched me as though I had betrayed a confidence.

'She told you that, did she?'

'Yes, I don't – '

'Well it's true: he went off when Peter was only just two.' Her anger confused me. Clearly, there was something I did not understand; something she thought her daughter might have told me but had not.

'Just two,' she repeated, smiling now, and nodding to herself. 'Mary was eleven, the eldest.'

I nodded.

'She's left school, you know.' She stopped abruptly, as if uncertain of how to continue, or of her reasons for announcing the fact.

'Yes, I know.'

'She'll be leaving soon. No work here – no prospects, you see.'

'Mother!' Mary released her grip on the boy and clenched her fists, pressing them against the concrete.

'The younger ones will be going back to school soon, I suppose,' I said, trying to ease the situation.

'School?' She looked down at the children, who had turned at my mention of the word. Only the small boy repeated it and looked uncertainly at us all.

'Yes, she said he thought you was his dad. He used to watch you from the window when you was on the site with the others.' Her tone was no longer accusatory, but her repetition of the fact made me angry, suggesting, I thought, that she believed I had encouraged the child in its mistake.

I nodded, looked at my watch and then at the open door of the lighthouse. 'There's another mist,' I said, pointing towards the sea and the charcoal-coloured smudge which hung offshore.

'It'll hold off,' she replied. 'In a fortnight, beginning of September, that's when they begin to come in.'

Ahead of us a door opened and Donald Owen appeared. He watched us for a moment before turning along the road and following the path into the dunes. She watched him, and I saw her smile. I turned to Mary, but she, too, was watching the man.

'Mister Owen,' the woman said absently, still watching as he descended the far slope, only his head and shoulders visible. Mary was the first to look away. Taking hold of her mother's arm, she pointed to me and said: 'He used to think that Mister Owen was our dad. I told him about Peter, and he said he thought Mister Owen was our dad. "Father," he called him.'

The woman turned to look at me, and from me to the point in the dunes where Donald Owen had disappeared. Mary watched her closely, smiling.

'Mister Owen?' she repeated, looking down at her daughter's hand.

I wanted to explain how innocent and short-lived my mistake had been, but I knew that once again anything I said would only serve to increase her anxiety.

Mary moved to stand behind me and announced that she thought it was time they went indoors. She took her mother's hand and led her towards the road, neither of them speaking to me as they passed. The children followed in a silent line.

I watched them, angry and confused by what the girl had said, by her deliberate cruelty towards us both.

At the door, Mary turned and waved. I did not respond and her waving become more vigorous and she began to laugh.

I sat where the woman had sat, lighting a cigarette and watching the houses through the fading light. Donald Owen returned from the dunes, pausing to look towards me before entering his own home.

I was, I suppose, the result of my parents' private celebration of the end of the Great War. But even this is not strictly true. I was born in January 1919, and must therefore have been conceived before the war's end. A year before my birth, my father had been wounded. A month prior to that he had received his inevitable promotion to major. It was not a permanent injury, but one which forced him away from the Front and back to his wife. After a month of convalescence, he was assigned to the task of organising transportation for new recruits. It was not a responsibility he enjoyed, and despite his promotion, the last months of his life were filled with frustration, guessing perhaps that the war would be fought to its conclusion without him.

Even before his death, our home was crowded with photographs of him in uniform, ribbons and insignia blossoming over his chest, head erect, eyes confident in the stability and permanence of the world which was shattering around him. The Army was his way of life; wars his recreation. His wife became little more than a distant relative, formally acknowledged and treated.

After his death, my future lay in the hands of the ranks of

uncles who closed around my mother. She became un-balanced and then withdrawn. She had loved and respected him far more than he had ever deserved. The uncles took upon themselves the responsibility for our welfare, my education, and the perpetuation of his memory.

I have often thought about the circumstances of my con-ception and birth, but now, with the death of my own son, there are too many uncomfortable parallels I would rather not acknowledge — parallels which seem to make his death so much more inevitable, and my own ability to have prevented it so much more obvious. She was thirty-five when she gave birth, he almost sixty.

Now I am forced to try and understand my own feelings and wonder at the balance of guilt and grief, at the useless domination of one over the other. The truth, I suppose, is that the demands made on the men of our family have resulted over the years in their inability to understand the needs of its other members, of its wives and children.

But just as the celebration of my own birth had proved eventually hollow, so too had my father's satisfaction at ensuring the continuation of the male line, of ensuring the continuity of a tradition which had long since usurped the ordinary feelings the members of a family might have for one another.

He saw me once before his death, and I remember him only through the silver-edged photographs: his arrogant, work-manlike face and confident smile. But perhaps it was not arrogance, only pride. Eventually, the photographs came to replace even my mother's memories.

I was born in January; he saw me in April and was killed in May, having chosen to return to Belgium as part of a legation dealing with the problems of the repatriation of prisoners and the release of businesses and buildings previously requisitioned for military purposes. An unexploded mine took his life along with seventeen others. In addition, forty-two men were injured in the blast. My father and six officers were post-humously decorated.

Fifty-nine injuries and deaths from a single blast. Even by comparison with the shells of the Second War, the figures seemed ridiculously high; even higher when compared to the charges designed solely to maim a single man, hidden in a car boot or overgrown hedge, carried by children or women with prams. But the mines had been designed honestly and simply to take as many lives as possible, rather than to attract attention to their taking. The explosion which killed Michael had not done its job properly: the man who twisted and set its trembling wires had not truly believed it capable of killing anyone, but simply in its value as a newsworthy propaganda device.

My own birth had been regarded by the uncles as a timely and fortuitous reminder of the strength of tradition. The fact that I was born a boy compounded their cause for celebration. I was there to occupy the time of a grieving widow; there, too, to embody the promise and potential of a father who would have wanted me to accomplish what they instructed her to do. She told me later that they had also insisted that I be taken to his funeral and held over the grave to see his coffin. I can remember nothing of the occasion, but realised later that the ornately fitted box would have contained very little, perhaps nothing, of his actual physical being.

The shock of his death and joy of my arrival worked against each other. Already considered old for childbearing, she began to relinquish control over me. She entered a period later described as 'her sickness'. She hired a succession of nannies and spent increasingly longer periods of time away from home, some of them in sanatoria. It was only later, as I prepared to leave school for university, that she began to regret what had happened and the distance which had been created between us. But by then it was too late: she had grown quickly old, and we were already living in a world on the slowly moving edge of yet another whirlpool.

Several of the uncles had died and great ceremonies had been made of their passing. The family foundered in their absence and in the absence of war. There were no nephews, and I alone rose as the disappointing bearer of what remained of any tradition. Others faded and died, unprepared for the changes taking place around them, the remainders of their families dispersing quickly into a secure and welcome anonymity. With each death and year of approaching senility, their grasp on me weakened. The last of them died a month after my mother in 1938, and having fought for so long to discard my past, my future became suddenly and unexpectedly empty and uncertain.

Rifle shots over a grave have always seemed to me to be obscene – a final celebration, confirmation that the military is relinquishing its grip on the body after it has served their purpose, as though even after death it has remained useful to them. The military presence at a funeral is not for the benefit of those who suffer genuine grief – for they would hardly notice – but for those peripheral witnesses who want to believe in something more heroic rather than to understand the circumstances of the death itself. There can be few things more final than a volley of gunfire over an open grave, few things more loaded with contradictory meanings than a line of rifles pointed Heavenwards.

I heard movements behind me and turned. She crossed the stone flags and stood at the edge of the lawn. I saw her breathe deeply, taking in the evening's scents. She touched the small white blooms beside her, smelling at her fingers, pulling at dead petals and clapping them from her hands.

'Do you like Mister Owen?' She asked the question as a young child would ask it, waiting for my simple or non-committal answer before delivering her own, more important response.

She sat beside the room's only window, studying a chart, feigning unconcern, ready to speak as I replied. I watched her, deliberately not answering. She looked up, impatiently at first, and then guiltily, tracing circles over the chart with her fingers. I knew what she wanted me to say, that she wanted to confirm my suspicions about her mother and the man. I knew also that anything I said stood a good chance of being repeated, and perhaps misinterpreted.

'I don't really think I know him well enough to be able to answer that.'

She pulled a face, her second question remaining unasked. Her annoyance betrayed a reassuring childish naivety. Realising that I understood why she had asked the question, she turned to the window and began to hum.

After a calculated silence, she spoke again: 'Sometimes I used to wish that my dad was dead and that he wasn't coming back.' She looked up. 'Do you know what I mean?'

'I think so.' My answer relaxed her.

'At first we thought he *was* dead. They sent a letter to say he was missing. And then after that they sent one to say he was alive. We thought he was dead for nearly two years.'

'That must have been a worrying – '

'They used to put lists in the newspapers. We used to have them sent so we could look for his name. I was only thirteen. When they knew where he was, we got another letter. At first she thought it was to tell her that he was dead. She took it straight round to show Mister Owen.' She looked up, waiting for my reaction. 'After that we got letters all the time. They even used to send us paper and envelopes with an address already on so that we could write back to him. We sent him some photos and stuff like that. He never used to write back, though.'

'And were you glad to hear that he was safe?'

She nodded. 'We saw pictures on the films. There was a ship with lots of black smoke and lines of soldiers, all waving. They told us where he was, but we didn't have a map. The place had a long name, and then they kept moving him about, so we never knew for certain where he was. Mister Christie said that they had to keep moving him because they were losing the war and had to keep running away. It's all desert islands where he was, see.'

I nodded; there would have been little point in disputing what she so firmly believed.

'At the school where we went, one of the girls' father was killed.' She left her seat to stand beside me at the table, lifting my arm to inspect a bandage where I had fallen and taken the skin from my elbow. 'Does it hurt?'

'No, not really; I only wear it for the sympathy it gets me.'

She laughed, tucking in the loose edges and turning my wrist to inspect my watch.

'I don't think I'll ever let my husband be a soldier,' she said seriously.

'God willing, he'll never have to be.'

'Won't there be any more wars, then?'

'I doubt it.'

'When he comes back, she . . .'

I waited. 'She what? Your mother, you mean?'

She nodded.

Outside, a tractor moved across a neighbouring field, and she turned to watch, both of us grateful for its interruption.

'We used to have picnics,' she said.

'Where, in the fields?'

'Sometimes. And sometimes we used to walk further than you can see and play in the river.'

'River? I didn't know there was a river.'

'Further than you can see.'

I started to roll up the plans.

'It looks bigger,' she said.

'Bigger?'

'Cable Point, the houses. It looks bigger when you see it all drawn out on paper. Which is our house?'

I showed her, and from it she began to identify the remaining buildings and features, pleased and excited at the prospect of being able to do so.

'When I've finished, I'll get you a copy of the map if you like. You can put it on the wall.' I expected the offer to please her, but she simply nodded, said 'Yes,' and began once again to inspect the frayed edge of my bandage.

five

She sat where I had first seen her on the day of my arrival. At my approach, she looked up. I stood at the crest of the dunes, watching a flock of terns perform their aerobatics, diving and disappearing in explosions of white. On either side of me, the strips of sloping sand and shingle ran like the parallel strokes of a single brush. Beneath me the remains of the foundations and their uprooted metal supports lay scattered like a spilled cargo, an abstract of greys and reds over the pale sand. Other, more distant flocks of birds rose and fell through the colour-less sky, and from my vantage point even the curve of the unbroken horizon seemed exaggerated.

'Sea swallows,' she said without turning.

'That's what you call them, is it?'

She nodded.

'I've just passed the others, rummaging about on the site.'

'They're just kids,' she said, still not turning to face me.

'Yes, I suppose so. I suppose you're getting too old for their games.' The remark was not entirely serious, but I was aware of how she felt and of the unwanted responsibilities being forced upon her by her age. To the older inhabitants she remained a child, caught between two worlds and confined by the isolation of the place.

'I *am* too old,' she answered indignantly.

'Perhaps when your father comes home and you start

work . . . perhaps then things might change. You're bound to make some new friends your own age. They must be crying out for bright' – I almost said girls – 'young women.'

She turned to watch me, flattered but suspicious. 'You think so?'

'Positive. You could get a job in Lincoln and perhaps even – '

'Oh.' She turned away and punched her fist into the soft sand. I had offered her a chance, and then, in my ignorance, taken it away.

On either side of us stretched the braid of weed, feathers and empty shells which marked the height of the previous night's tide. She inspected a crab shell, balancing and spinning it on her finger before snapping it easily in half and letting it fall.

'Perhaps your father will get a job somewhere else and you'll all move with him.'

'Away from here, you mean? Further than Lincoln?'

'Yes. Why? Don't you want to leave?'

She laughed contemptuously, as though leaving Cable Point was the sole aim of her life. Picking up a handful of pebbles, she threw them into the calm water, watching as the confused ripples melted flat.

'She says that we'll probably have to move whatever happens. She says they won't let him work at the new station. Will they?'

Clearly, she still believed I had some authority over who was to be employed at the new site. For her sake, I decided to lie.

'I'm not sure. Perhaps when they realise he used to work on the boats before the war, perhaps then they'll be able to find him a job.'

She didn't believe me, and turned away. I wanted to leave. She opened her legs, burying her hands in the shingle between them, watching it settle and roll into the sea.

'We had a body during the war,' she said, raising her arms and tilting them to dislodge the last of the pebbles.

'A body! Where?'

'Right here.' She patted the space between her legs.

'What sort of body?'

'I don't know – just a body. Some soldiers came in a lorry and took him away. Mister Christie said it was a sailor from a boat that had been sunk. He didn't have any clothes on – just wellingtons. They just came and took him off. Mister Owen said he was a German.' She spoke calmly, smiling to herself, making me doubt the truth of what she said.

'That must have been quite a shock for you all.'

She shrugged. 'I found him, me. It was me who saw him first. I saw him from up there.' She pointed over her shoulder to the dunes.

'And they came to take him away?'

She nodded again. 'Mister Christie said that if he was a German then he deserved all he got. Him and the others came down until the soldiers got here.'

'Others?'

'The other men. They made us wait up at the top. All we could see was his legs. They couldn't get the lorry past the end of the road and so they had to carry him in a blanket. Mister Owen made us all go into the houses until they'd gone. He said the birds had been at him.' She recounted the incident without emotion, and without the excited embellishments most other children might have added. I was convinced she was lying.

'I suppose they took him away for burial,' I said. But what I thought did not interest her. She simply shrugged and continued throwing pebbles into the sea.

Further along the beach two men appeared, climbing over the row of small upturned boats, scraping at their bleached wooden hulls. She turned to watch and I stood to leave. As I did so, she said:

'We had another body – where the guns were.'

'What! On the gun site? Are you certain?' Now I knew she was lying, and wondered at her motives. She turned to face me, looking up and shielding her eyes, hiding them.

I asked her to show me the precise location of the second body. She agreed, and walked beside me towards the houses, brushing the dust from her arms and legs. The men by the boats stopped to watch us. She tried to whistle. I became convinced that I was about to become the victim of a hoax and that she would suddenly burst into laughter and run off.

'Someone killed during the war, you mean?'

'I don't know.'

'So it wasn't while you were here, then?'

'No; before.'

I smiled to myself, reassured by her uncertainty. As we left the narrow path through the brambles, she held my hand.

'Show me from here,' I said as we began to descend, pointing over the entire site beneath us.

'I can't. You can't see it because of all the rubbish.'

'Yes, of course.'

At the edge of the road she stopped. 'Will they really give my dad his job back?'

I said that I honestly didn't know. This satisfied her and she crossed onto the site.

'Did the soldiers come for this one, too?'

'No – it's still buried.'

'Still buried! That should be something for us to keep an eye out for!' My mocking tone made her angry and she moved ahead of me, climbing easily over the broken concrete blocks, waiting impatiently for me to catch up with her.

'Right, where is it?' I asked, standing beside her on the remains of a sunken doorway.

'Under there,' she said, pointing down without looking.

I looked down and recognised the trench in which the man's legs had been crushed, and in which he had lain helpless, screaming and then unconscious.

She waited for my reaction, smiled to herself, and then jumped down, leaving me alone at the centre of the empty site, remembering the man's forced cheerfulness as he exhibited the sewn pyjama legs laid empty across his hospital bed.

A line of men lay hidden in the shadow of the bomber's remaining wing. Along the fuselage a line of almost thirty shell holes had been ringed with scarlet paint, awaiting the repair which never came. Above each circle was a painted number. The paint had run before drying, leaving the impression of bleeding wounds.

The driver of the lorry in which I rode pointed to the men and swore. They shouted back, exaggerating their American accents, laughing at their jokes and at the driver's frustrated gestures to them. Two older men sat apart, standing as we approached and crossing the open runway to meet us. They were both fat men, wiping their necks and collecting the sweat from their faces in the palms of their hands. They walked slowly, unconcerned, tiring in the heat and waving down the continued shouting of the men beneath the wing.

They introduced themselves and said they had been expecting us. I handed down the requisition order for the pump we had come to collect. They each read the sheet, half turned and began to recite a list of names. Those called emerged reluctantly into the sunlight. Others refused to come, and the two men – both sergeants – smiled apologetically before shouting again, their tone more serious. They continued to shout, swear and applaud as the men ran toward us. They stopped beside the lorry, formed into a line and saluted, perfectly synchronised, their fingers barely touching their temples. The two sergeants returned the gesture, and the men relaxed, continuing to complain at the heat and what they were being ordered to do. The sergeants mimicked them and laughed.

Together, we walked to the edge of the runway where a petrol-driven pump splashed water from an overgrown drain onto the warm concrete.

The Americans were restless and bored, anxious to return home, left in the wake of the aircrew – non-combatants whose own return could clearly wait. Because of this they resented every imposition and demand made upon them. The sergeants berated them, the men laughed, and a very fine balancing act was maintained between relaxed control and what, in the British Army, would almost certainly have been regarded as insubordination.

A hand-operated winch was dragged to the drain, and we

began the process of lifting the pump onto the lorry. Afterwards, I accepted the sergeants' offer of a cold drink. The
driver, too, was invited, but he chose to remain in his cab,
exposed to the heat, the air around him thick with petrol
fumes.

The sergeants introduced themselves and we exchanged
brief histories of what we had done and what we were doing.
Our conversation was neatly divided into what had happened
during the war and what had – or hadn't – happened since.
They disguised their own disappointment at having to remain,
complaining instead on behalf of the men. They had known the
gun crews stationed at Cable Point, and had visited there to
swim in the sea. I invited them back, but they shook their
heads, saying they had orders to remain on the base. On their
frequent weekend leaves, they explained, they were still
allowed to travel, but mostly this was in the direction of
Lincoln, or southwards towards Grantham and the other
sprawling bases with their abandoned communities awaiting
their own return home. Besides which, they considered
themselves unwelcome at Cable Point, particularly since the
return of the small resident population. I asked them why,
but they could not explain. Intuition, one said. The other
nodded. It was just the way people reacted, they explained,
to seeing them still there. 'Reminds folk too much of the
war.' Both shrugged, unconcerned, agreeing with everything
the other said. Nevertheless, I repeated my invitation and
they both promised to come.

From the all-round view of the control tower I could see
the runways extending in each direction, their ends obscured
by the haze as they cut through the level fields of growing
crops which surrounded them. I pointed down to the aircraft
under which the men sat. This plane, the sergeants proudly
informed me, had been the last to crash-land, a fortnight
after the end of the war. It had been dragged clear and had
remained where it lay for over a year. I remembered the aircraft which had lost its tailplane, and wondered if it, too, had
been stationed here.

'Had a lot of fuck-ups immediately after they stopped flying missions,' one of them said, his use of the swear word betraying no emotion, only the difference between us.

'They get sloppy, get restless. It happens.'

'Yes, I suppose so.'

They nodded, looking down at their hands, a shared memory.

'Just get careless, I guess.' The man shrugged, holding up his palms. The other nodded, and both turned to look down at the broken aircraft, and then at the others and the precise spaces between them.

'You hear about the Fort crash?'

I nodded.

They shook their heads and turned away from each other. One of them took off his cap and wiped his hand down his face, holding it out to watch the sweat drip from his finger.

She moved easily across the scattered rubble and shifting blocks, following a course along which our paths would intersect.

It was early evening, and a light breeze blew in off the sea, the bank of low mist threatening to follow. There were a number of names for both the mists and the winds depending on their speed, direction, the amounts of water they held or the time of year at which they arrived. My mistakes were quietly corrected and never the source of amusement.

She steadied herself against the wind, holding her arms like an acrobat and rocking the blocks of stone and concrete as she moved over them. The material of her dress clung to her body, billowing and falling behind her. I saw both the girlish thinness of her legs and the beginnings of those of a woman. She was once again barefoot, testing each step before committing herself. She saw me watching, and paused, pretending not to have seen.

I left the end of the road and continued through the blowing sand towards the Light. She began to move more swiftly, unable to hide her urgency.

We exchanged our usual casual greeting and I asked her about the mist, and whether or not it was expected to move inland. She seemed unconcerned, said that it was unlikely, and began to ask me about the day's work. I made a joke and she laughed loudly, stopping abruptly and looking back to the row of houses, in which the first of the evening's lights had appeared. She offered to come into the lighthouse and make a pot of tea. I accepted because I could not have refused without offending her or indicating to her that I understood the contrived nature of our meeting. She crossed the short distance between us and slid her arm through mine. This, too, seemed to have been a carefully planned manoeuvre. She smiled up at me, and I found myself unable and unwilling to extricate myself. In wartime London, women had frequently slid their arms into mine – largely for their benefit rather than mine. The secretaries and drawing-room assistants did it, as did the women from the driving pool. They held their bended arms out and smiled, maintaining their distance by talking continuously, mentioning their husbands or fiancés on active service. Their hands were often gloved, resting limply, making no contact other than touching.

We passed behind the low wall of the old coastguard station. Now she held me with both hands, her head against my arm. I could not prevent myself from looking down. She, in turn, was careful not to look up. At the lighthouse, she withdrew and ran ahead of me, waiting breathless at the door.

'It's open. Go straight in.'

She pushed the door open, but waited for me to enter ahead of her, as though there might have been something inside of which she was afraid. I dropped my charts and she asked me about them, circling the small room and nodding uninterestedly as I explained. There were times during all our conversations when she seemed completely uncertain of herself, as though she had formed only a single plan or prepared for only a single topic of discussion, becoming annoyed at my innocent diversions. The act of making the tea seemed to reassure her and she began to reply, asking me about what

I was doing and telling me about life at Cable Point prior to her temporary evacuation from it. On both subjects she seemed equally unconcerned with my answers and with her own feelings about the changes taking place around her. It was as though she had already decided to leave, and that nothing that happened now had any bearing on her future away from the place.

Occasionally, she asked about my past, angry when I refused to be drawn, or when my answer contradicted what she wanted to hear. Here, too, I felt as though I was being manipulated, forced into either lying or exchanging personal details for those about her own past which meant nothing to her.

She brought the pot to the table, moving it in almost imperceptible circles, the motion transferring to her shoulders and the loose material of her dress.

'Your father will be home in less than a week.'

' "Father"? Oh, dad. Yes, Friday.'

I knew the date from her mother. The letter had contained the details of his journey and time of arrival. After such a long wait, she had become confused, needing to confirm each detail – first with Donald Owen, and then with me. Only I, it seemed, had discussed the event with her and listened to her anxieties, many of which she could find neither the confidence nor words to express. I wondered about her neighbours' reluctance to become involved with the man's return. When she did speak of her fears and uncertainties, she did so only to encourage my reassurances. On one occasion I had mentioned Donald Owen. She had stopped abruptly, studying her hands and then my face for an indication of what I might have guessed or been told. Afterwards, she had apologised, telling me that he had been a great help to both her and the children. I assured her that I understood, but she still studied my face, looking around us to see which, if any, of the neighbours had been watching and might have overheard.

The following day she had avoided me, moving quickly into the dark shadow of her home as I left the Light.

'They're bringing him all the way from London in a car. All

the way – just him in a car with a driver.' She poured the tea, watching the liquid as she spoke.

'So they should,' I said. 'He deserves it.'

She looked up to judge the sincerity of what I said, and smiled. 'We were going to write to the coastguard people to see if we could use the downstairs of number two.'

'Number two?'

'The one next door, where the ceiling's fallen in. She said we could perhaps use it for a bedroom.' She shrugged, unconvinced of the likelihood of that happening. I realised then the overcrowding likely to be caused by her father's return, knowing of the cramped conditions in which the woman and two children already lived.

'I don't see why not.' I avoided her eyes, knowing it unlikely that any such repair would be carried out.

She shook her head. 'We haven't written yet. She was only talking about it. That's all she ever does. She says it's too far to send the builders and that we couldn't afford the rent.'

'I daresay you'll manage. You must have managed before he went away.'

She nodded, leaving her seat to once again circle the room. 'Mister Christie had a cellar for keeping fish.'

'A cellar?'

She banged her foot on the square of carpet beneath the table. 'There's a trapdoor.'

During the previous weeks, I had often seen the men standing in a line along the shingle, casting lines into the sea. These they fastened with stakes into the dunes, or to the rusted supports protruding from the embankment. Occasionally, they made me gifts of any surplus the night might have brought. In return I offered them cigarettes, but they seemed genuinely unconcerned about making any exchange, taking what was offered purely as a favour to me. Only the women ever made a fuss of thanking me for whatever I might be able to give them from my stores.

'Did – does your father fish?'

She shrugged. 'They all do.' She came to sit on the arm of

71

my chair. 'Do you want to see a picture?' Her hand moved towards her pocket, waiting. This, I realised, had been the true purpose of her visit.

'Of your father, you mean?'

'Dad. Yes.' She took out a frayed card wallet, on the cover of which her father's name had been written in pencil. She held it as I read the name, waiting for my nod of approval. Inside was a photograph sandwiched between two pieces of tissue.

'We made it when he first went off,' she said.

I took out the picture of the man's face and chest.

'That's his uniform.' She moved closer, swinging her legs across my own. The picture was beginning to fade, its white border dirty and weakened with constant handling.

The man was smiling broadly, one eye half closed against the sun or in a wink; his mouth open revealing his teeth. There was an obvious pride in the way his chin was held above his buttoned jacket, and his black beret with its single indistinguishable badge sat at a perfect angle. He looked no older than twenty-two or three, but from the date on the reverse – 1940 – I knew him to be at least thirty.

'He looks to have made a good soldier,' I said, smiling at the differences between his face and the serious poses of my own father. She took the photograph and nodded – as though the compliment had been intended for her and not him. She then returned it carefully to its folder and slid it back into her pocket.

She left me to climb onto the stool beneath the small window, pulling herself onto the deep sill and looking out into the growing darkness. She twisted herself around in the small space until she sat looking down at me.

'Do you think he was a good soldier even though he surrendered?' she asked seriously.

'Yes, I do. He didn't surrender because he was frightened or anything: he was ordered to surrender along with thousands of others. They surrendered because there was nothing else they could do.'

She nodded, but seemed unwilling to continue. 'Mister Christie said he would have gone to Dunkirk if the boats had still been here.'

'I daresay he would have done,' I said, making no attempt to hide the contempt I had come to feel for the man.

'Were you at Dunkirk?'

I laughed. 'No, I'm afraid not.'

'Where were you, then?'

'Oh, various places. North Africa, Italy, and then later, afterwards, in Germany.'

'Hitler's Germany? Nazi Germany?' she said, repeating the popular headlines.

'Yes, I suppose so. But that was afterwards, when – ' I tensed, remembering something I had wanted to forget.

'Will you come and see him when he gets home? Will you come and talk to him? Nobody else here was in the war.' The question surprised me. I felt ashamed of my resentment, and then flattered. This is what the photograph had been a prelude to.

'Yes, of course I'll come. But I think you ought to ask – '

'It was *her* idea,' she said quickly. 'She said that if you came to see him, then perhaps he might . . .' She dropped from the sill and walked to the door.

I watched her as she returned to the houses, their squares of light casting long shadows over the broken ground. From beyond the buildings, somewhere amongst the dunes, came the tuneless, frantic sound of a harmonica.

Just as there had been accidents during the construction of the fortifications, so there were several during their demolition. There were none as tragic as the man's crushed legs, but ones which nonetheless added to the growing resentment of the labour force as they continued with their arduous and – to them – seemingly unnecessary task. Already they had expressed their criticisms of the work schedule and the thoroughness with which the beds of steel and concrete were to be dismantled. It was their restlessness and carelessness, added to the nature of the work, which was responsible for the accidents. I discussed their grievances with them, and realised that it was not so much the task itself which they resented, but the fact that they considered themselves to have been forgotten, destined to continue as they had always done. I sympathised with them: the public needed no more heroes to welcome home, just the opportunity to forget.

I wrote to my own superiors, requesting that the period of demolition be extended. This was refused. The work, it was suggested, 'should continue to be undertaken with the enthusiasm and commitment previously devoted to the War Effort'. It was an easy thing to say, and perhaps the person who had written it believed that we would respond to its stimulus. I read the letter to them as they awaited the arrival of the lorries. They understood their helplessness only too well and nodded solemnly.

The most serious of the accidents occurred when the bar being used to lever a block from its supports slipped and trapped a man's hand. He screamed, partly in pain, but mostly at his fear of how the injury might leave him. Fortunately, the block was easily removed. The broken hand began to colour and swell, covered in blood where the skin had been scraped from it. We went in a group to the houses, where it was washed, spread with foul-smelling ointment and fastened in a simple bandage. I tested each finger, judging by his suppressed cries which were broken. The others laughed, relieved at the nature of the injury, reassuring him and then themselves. The woman who had applied the bandage informed us that her father's arm had been broken on no fewer than six separate occasions, caught in the winding gear of the boats. As further consolation, she added that he had lived until eighty.

The men moved back into the workings. I swore at them, accusing them of carelessness. They avoided my eyes and nodded guiltily.

It was in Germany, Bonn, that I met my wife in the summer of 1947. She was working as an auxiliary nurse, alternating between a hospital in the process of being built and the one being demolished beside it. We were married two years later, continuing to spend long periods apart. Michael was born in 1951. She retired from nursing and returned with him to Oxfordshire to establish our first real home. I was able to return frequently, but it was not until 1959, when Michael was eight, that I was finally stationed in London, making the daily journey by train. But even then I knew that important bonds had not been formed, and that I missed something vital. Increasingly, I came to regard the two of them as something separate – as a single unit living apart from me. Perhaps it was for that reason that I volunteered to return on a year's assignment to Germany, and following that Gibraltar and Aden. By then, the actual physical distances between us had become unimportant.

At first I made excuses. Later, there was no need. My ideas about how I wanted them to be and feel about me became something with which I continued to deceive myself as we grew further apart. And as we parted so the self-deceptions became easier.

Michael was thirteen when I returned permanently to Oxfordshire. She informed me of the career she had planned for him – or, rather, the one she was determined he should avoid. We tried to reconcile our feelings for his sake, but our emotions became destructive. After that, our marriage became a cold ritual, creating even more deceptions which neither of us was brave or strong enough to want to destroy.

It was only later that I understood how much I was to blame for what had happened. After that, things became easier – as though we had somehow reached a plateau upon which our feelings had exhausted themselves.

Michael rebelled against her plans, and I mistook it for a personal victory, not realising then that my own wishes for his future had been identical to her own.

Afterwards, when we were alone and waiting for news, we began to sift through what had happened, moving slowly back together in the process.

six

Why had my father returned so unnecessarily to Belgium so soon after my birth? It is a question to which I have provided countless answers, each less satisfying than the last. Perhaps it was simply that the prospect of becoming a father unsettled or threatened him – he was, after all, almost sixty. Or perhaps he believed that the war to end all wars would live up to its claim and leave him without a purpose in life. Perhaps he could not tolerate the thought of a life without the military strictures and certainties in which he had been moulded. Or perhaps he had become careless, anxious at the uncertainty and changes in his own life and in the world around him. Perhaps my mother forced him away, accepting and then demanding his long absences. From what I had learned as I grew, their relationship had suffered the same strains I was later to impose on my own marriage.

My very first memory was of being surrounded by uni-formed men – my uncles and close family friends, I suppose – and of being passed from hand to hand, held up and inspected. It had been hot, and I remember the perambulator with its fringe of white and another peering woman, heavily clothed despite the heat. Then she had stood away, and I had cried as the hands continued to fondle and inspect me. My father was not present, and perhaps he was already dead.

My second memory is of a parade, and of being held by my

mother at the front of a mass of people, watching lines of soldiers in dress uniform and lorries drawing small guns. She had pointed, and around us everyone had cheered. I think I was seeing the King. Bands played and other children stood alone, some of them with flags, all of them cheering. My greatest fear on that occasion was that she would release her grip on my shoulders and that I should be separated from her and lost.

Even now I do not know what the occasion for the ceremony had been, only that we had been alone, and that I had cried to return home as she had wandered through the crowded streets, seemingly not caring whether I held her or not.

The woman moved around the cramped interior of the room, collecting crockery and talking to me via Mary who stood beside the window and said nothing more than was demanded of her. I sat on the overstuffed sofa which took up too much space in the small house. I was asked about the work and about the changes being made. She asked out of politeness, neither of them interested in my answers. I answered the woman directly, shouting through into the even smaller kitchen into which she had gone. Mary watched me, eager to leave, embarrassed by her mother's questions and awkward conversation. On the floor beside the hearth the small boy lay asleep.

The room was refreshingly cool. Through the open window I saw the grey and white of the demolition site, and beyond that the vivid yellow of the adjoining field.

Mary, I guessed, had been told to remain indoors whilst I was there. Silently, she attracted my attention, spelling out a word with her finger, stopping abruptly as her mother re-entered the room, wiping her hands on her apron.

As the days to her husband's return passed, her anxiety had become increasingly evident. She began to isolate herself, remaining indoors during the daytime and keeping herself apart from the other women as they gathered each evening. They, in turn, responded by moving away from the houses, some-times following their husbands to sit amongst the broken buildings and piles of rubble. The small boy still made his demands, but increasingly she had relinquished his control to her daughter.

She sat beside me, repeating things I had told her daughter about myself. I watched Mary as her mother spoke, but she seemed unconcerned at what I might have thought about the confidences she had repeated. She remained silent, only nodding each time the woman turned for confirmation of what she was repeating.

'Mary says they'll be bringing in new men for the station. Says the old crews won't be able to work the boat. She says they're putting in a new light.'

My previously guarded answers had become solid facts, something I was now unable to deny, and something every one of the inhabitants would have known about.

Then Mary spoke for the first time. 'He says they'll build a brand-new station and that the coastguard people won't ever mend next door.' There was no malice in her voice, and she was smiling.

The woman looked at me, but there was nothing I could say to reassure her.

'We could use the space, you see,' she said, as though the decision on the repairs was still mine to make. I shook my head, and she looked down, signalling her hopelessness.

Silence followed in which Mary watched us both.

'I showed him the photo,' she said, waiting for her mother's response.

After that, the woman began to talk about her husband, asking the questions already asked by her daughter.

I tried to answer her honestly, grateful that I knew neither the man nor the details of what he had endured. Above all else, she wanted reassurance.

I was shown more photographs, and Mary sat beside me, between us, taking them from her mother and holding them for me to see. She, too, began to ask more questions, repeating ones I had already answered. The photographs had all been taken within a short time of each other, and in almost all of them the man was in uniform, always smiling for the camera, his chin up and his arms either folded across his chest or held stiffly by his side.

When we had finished, I was told how old he had been, shown the most recent picture again, and asked if I thought he would be much changed. I said that four years was a long time and that anybody would have changed. She seemed satisfied. I could have made other, more optimistic guesses, but there can have been little that she had not already considered. I tried to sound hopeful. She thanked me and replaced the photos in the box from which they had been taken.

'But you think there'll be work for him on the new station?' She asked it and turned away, smiling at her daughter as though wanting to believe what *she* had told her and not what I might say.

The child on the floor rolled over and awoke, turning to face us as we looked down. Mary pursed her lips at him and he laughed.

The woman returned to the kitchen.

Mary watched her, and then, unexpectedly, turned to me and said in a voice intended to be heard, 'You should have told her what you told me.' The accusation caught me unawares. In the kitchen, the woman stopped and turned to look.

The child held out its arms, and Mary knelt to caress him.

I wanted to demand an explanation, to explain to the woman that I knew as little as she. Instead, I left, shouting my unacknowledged farewell from the doorway.

Later that same evening, they stood together beside the road, the shadow of the houses hiding their faces. As I passed they nodded formally, waiting for me to move away before resuming their conversation.

The following morning, Mary appeared at the lighthouse.

'She says she's sorry – about last night.' She waited in the doorway, stepping backwards into the light as I approached her. We watched each other, both assessing our reactions.

'Did she send you?'

She hesitated. With the light from behind it was difficult to see the expression on her face.

'Or have you come on your own accord to apologise for your own behaviour?'

She shrugged and looked down, watching her bare feet as she stepped forward.

'She said afterwards that she was sorry, that we shouldn't have bothered you.'

I tried to determine whether or not she was telling the truth. I decided she was, but that once again she was using it to suit her own purposes.

'She said we'd just have to wait and see, and make the best of a bad job. Said that if we had to move, then there was nothing we could do about it.' Even in her daughter's repetition of her phrases, the woman's helplessness remained evident.

'Are you coming in?' I asked.

She walked into the room and stood with her hands together.

'It's not going to be easy for her, Mary – not after all this time. You're the only one who's going to be of any real practical help to her.'

'I know. She said.'

'It'll be up to you to make things easier by – '

She began to nod, willing me to stop. I was telling her things she had been told a dozen times, and which she probably resented. She remained standing, contrite, avoiding my face.

'Why did you make your mother think I was lying to her?'

'When?' She shouted the word, genuinely surprised and angry.

'Last night. You said that I should have told her what I'd already told you. What did you mean?'

She shrugged.

'Don't try and tell me that you've forgotten – you said it deliberately and loudly so that she would overhear.'

'You told her lies!'

'I told her exactly the same as I'd told you.'

'Yes, but – '

'But what?'

'But when you said it to her, it sounded as if you were lying. When you told me, it was like you were telling the truth.'

'It was the truth, Mary.' I moved towards her, speaking more quietly. 'I told her what I did because I don't know any more than she does, than you do.'

She watched me. 'So we will have to move away when they build the new station?'

'Mary, I honestly don't know. If I – '

'That's what she said. We'll probably have to go to Lincoln or somewhere like that.'

'But you wouldn't mind that, would you?'

'I don't suppose so.'

'I thought you wanted to get away from here, get a job . . . a husband.'

She smiled at the last word and became as shy and defensive as any fifteen-year-old girl would have become.

'I wouldn't mind moving away,' she said eventually, 'but I suppose we'll have to see what happens first.'

'Happens?'

'With my dad. The letter said that he'd probably still have to go into the hospital in Lincoln – not to stay, just for medicine and stuff. He's been in a year. They can't make him stay in any longer, can they?'

'I suppose it's just to keep a check on him; to make sure he's recovering as well as he should be.'

She nodded and moved to the seat beneath the window, closing her eyes and turning her face to the block of sunlight which crossed the floor and climbed the wall.

'Tell me the truth, Mary. Did your mother really send you across to apologise?'

She shook her head, her eyes still closed. 'No, but she did say afterwards that she was sorry.'

'I see.'

'She would have sent me across, I'm sure. Only she said we weren't to bother you.'

'But you must have known that what you said would have hurt her.'

She shrugged, still refusing to open her eyes. 'I had a magazine with a picture of a woman – a model – who had a neck like this.' She lifted her chin and stroked her neck with the back of her hand. 'And a tan all over.' She tilted her head and sucked in her cheeks.

'You must talk about your father's return quite a lot.'

But she refused to be drawn, turning her other cheek to the sun. 'She had sunglasses with white frames pointed at the ends.' She drew the outline of the glasses over her eyes. I wanted to accuse her of having been deliberately cruel, for her to confess. 'We had some shoes in a catalogue, once. Like sandals, but with pointed toes and long heels.'

What had she hoped to achieve? Was it because of what her father's return meant with regard to her own independence? Or was it something between her and her mother I did not yet understand?

'Why do you always call him "father"?' She had stopped posing, and was watching me.

'What?'

'You always call him my "father". Is that what you call your own?'

'Yes, it is.'

'And is he in the Army?'

I nodded.

'We always call him "dad". Always have done.'

'But you call your mother "mother".'

'I suppose so. Do you call yours "mother"?'

I nodded again, and she laughed.

'She used to tell us that when he did come back, he'd have presents for us all. She said he'd have stuff like silk and coconuts. Have you ever seen a coconut?'

I told her that I hadn't, not even in North Africa, where I had mistakenly believed them to grow.

'I've seen them in books,' she said, almost as if trying to cheer me up. She went on to describe them, and I listened and nodded as though I had never known.

'I don't suppose he will have any presents, will he? Especially not after all this time.'

I shook my head. 'He might have done,' I said, 'but four years is a long time. I don't suppose even a coconut would last that long.'

She agreed with me, and then asked me what London was like.

I told her detail after useless detail, and she nodded eagerly at them all.

After an hour she prepared to leave.

'Will you tell her that I've been?' she asked.

'Do you want me to?'

But she simply shrugged and walked out into the brilliant sunshine.

seven

There had been a ceremony, a Passing-Out parade at which we had sat together, temporarily reunited in our pride, looking down from the scaffolding of cloth-covered seating to the playing bands and marching squares. She had been disappointed at being unable to recognise him amongst so many identical faces and bodies. She had been proud then, despite her objections to the life to which he was committing himself. She had cried and held my hand, and I was reminded of Germany and the summer we met.

My own feelings of pride had been unexpected, leaving me uncertain but relieved at the thought that he had finally achieved a measure of independence. Around us, a thousand other mothers cried and their husbands held their hands, searching for their own anonymous sons.

Afterwards, as we walked with him and shook countless hands, I wanted her to admit that she had been wrong: to confess to us both that what he was doing, he was doing for the right reasons, and that it was his achievement, not hers or mine.

He had travelled home with us, still in uniform. She held his cap, balancing it on her head for us to see and laugh at. Three years ago, but I can still remember every gesture and word.

He showed us more photographs of himself and others, in

and out of uniform, uncontained smiles breaking their serious faces. She chose her favourite and he insisted that she keep it. In one he was a boy holding a can from which a blur of shaken froth spouted. In another his eyes were hidden in the shadow of his cap and he was a man in uniform, upright, emotionless. Later, I looked at photographs of myself at the same age. In those, too, I progressed from a boy to a man, standing beside an uncle in a badly-fitting jacket, hands on my hips. In others I wore loose white trousers and smiled foolishly, preoccupied with manhood yet undeniably young.

She asked him about his postings over the coming year and he told her he did not yet know. It was the first of his necessary lies. I saw her tense, believing he was keeping something from her. He insisted it was the truth, but after that she was never fully relaxed. She told him she believed him, and for a fortnight, with her son at home, she was content.

Later, as we sat alone, I wanted to warn him against what might lie ahead of him, of the easy, often irresistible choices with which he would be confronted.

Looking back, that first fortnight we spent together as a family was the most fulfilling I have spent as a father and husband. It was only later, as he confirmed his postings, that our relationship began once again to deteriorate. Then she accused me of having known all along, of encouraging him to keep things from her just as I had done. During his first tour, her obsessive anxiety became the barrier to any further reconciliation. Even during his subsequent periods at home, we were never able to recapture the security and optimism of that first fortnight. He, too, sensed that something was once again wrong, and increasingly he began to spend parts of his leave elsewhere. On one occasion, he spent less than a week with us and almost a fortnight with a girl in London.

She would never admit to it, but it was then – and to a girl and not the Army – that he was finally lost to us. In some ways it was easier to let her go on believing that the Army had taken him from us and for her to blame me for what had happened.

There were times when every evening news report contained the details of another killing or fresh atrocity, and she would listen with her hands clenched into fists, as though this would in some way prepare her for what she might hear. For her sake, I tried to appear unconcerned, but this only alienated her further. She accused me of not caring and began to bait me with questions of how I would react when it was his name they read out, when it was him they were describing. Sometimes I left the house and walked, but more often I sat only a few feet from her and absorbed her contempt and accusations. Our fears for his safety were identical, but by exposing them daily she made it seem all the more likely that they would be realised. When it did happen there was no television report, just the few lines in the unopened newspaper on the lawn.

The children banged their palms against the door, shouted my name and ran away. I heard them against the opposite side of the tower, leaping and shouting through the small window. At first I thought it to be another of their games, but looking out I saw the two American sergeants from Walsham.

They wore shorts and canvas shoes, with wide, loose shirts, brightly coloured and open to their stomachs. I shouted to them and they turned, uncertain of where my voice had come from. The smaller children formed into a row ahead of me, watching the two men and ready to run at their approach. Attracted by the noise, the women came to their doorways, looked out and withdrew. The men waited at the road's end. Mary and her mother came out and stood in their garden The men shouted to them, but neither of them answered, Mary simply pointing to where I stood. They turned and saw me, each of them waving and shouting with relief.

One of them carried a wicker basket, and both balanced fishing rods on their shoulders. I beckoned them towards me across the sand and concrete debris. The children parted at their approach, closing behind them and walking single file in their wake. The man with the basket dropped it and shook my hand. Both were sweating heavily in the heat, their arms and faces coated with dust.

'You walked?'

They turned to look back along the road, its sides closing to a point which remained invisible in the rising haze.

'From the junction; we hitched a ride as far as that.' He waved his arms vaguely in the direction taken by the unseen road.

The women reappeared in their doorways, Mary and her mother still watching us from where they stood. I raised my arm and some of the women waved back, gathering together to discuss what was happening and why the two strangely dressed men had arrived.

'They don't see many strange faces,' I explained, apologising for their reception.

They exchanged a glance and a smile. 'We heard.'

'Have you been fishing here before?' I nodded to the rods.

'Drove over a couple of years back – '

'But there weren't nobody around then – just some anti-aircraft outfit.' He pronounced it 'ant-eye' with the emphasis on the first syllable. The other nodded in confirmation. Behind them, the children moved closer, speculating loudly and collecting around the canvas rod bags and the basket, inspecting them at arm's length with their slender canes. The smallest child, Mary's brother, approached and stood between the men, staring up at them, at their exposed legs. A girl shouted him back, but he remained where he was.

'They've come from over at Walsham,' I said to the girl. 'Come to do some fishing.' I pointed towards the sea and they turned to look. 'They're nothing to do with the lighthouse or coastguard; they're just some friends of mine.' I added this in the hope that it would be conveyed to the watching women who strained to hear what was being said.

'They're from the coastguard people,' the girl shouted. Those around her nodded solemnly. I saw Mary turn to her mother and slide an arm around her waist. I wanted to shout and explain.

The two men looked at each other, puzzled. 'Coastguards?'

'They're going to build a new station here when all this is finished. They think you're part of all that.'

'So why the sour looks?'

'Well, the chances are that the men already living here who worked at the old station will be replaced.' I spoke in a low voice, anxious not to be overheard by the girl. She watched us suspiciously, shouting once again to the small boy still beside us. The men laughed, and she repeated her assertion that they were from the coastguard. The others took up the cry, their shouts fading as one of the men took a packet from his shirt and handed it down to the boy, who held it in his open palm, looking from the man to me.

'Gum?' I asked.

The man shook his head. 'Chocolate. Least that's what they call it.' They both laughed.

The girl approached us, looked up at the two men and snatched the packet from the boy's open hand. She unwrapped it cautiously and announced its contents to the others, causing them to rush forward and claim their share. The man took out a second packet, hesitated, sighed, patted his stomach and laughed. Mary left her mother, and the children ran towards her to display their prize. Her mother waited beside the gate, both hands resting on the wall. We left the children and went into the lighthouse.

'You tearing all this up?'

'Most of it.'

'The guns gone?'

'Yes, long since.'

We lit cigarettes, filling the room with smoke. They exchanged a signal, and from the basket pulled out a dozen bottles of beer, complaining at their warmth before standing them in the shadows around the room.

'Fish yourself? We brought a pole.'

I admitted that I didn't. They offered to teach me, laughing at a joke I did not understand. I accepted, glad of the opportunity to spend a day in their company. I explained in greater detail about what was happening at Cable Point, about the feelings of the people who lived there, and about the return of the woman's husband. They thought it strange that I should prefer to remain on the site rather than return to Lincoln each night with the others.

'They slapped a Prohibited Access beyond the junction when the local population returned,' one of them said.

'Out of Bounds, you mean?'

'That's it: "Out of Bounds".' He mimicked my accent and we all laughed.

'Beats me why anyone would want to live here in the first place.'

The other nodded his agreement, flicking his stub of cigarette through the open door.

'We used to use the light as a stager for incomings.'

'Oh?'

He nodded, thinking that I understood.

'Yeah. See that beautiful light for twenty miles over the ocean.'

'Ocean?'

'Sea. The North Sea.'

They told me about themselves: they were third-generation Americans, one of Polish and one of German extraction. Both came from Iowa – 'Place called Spencer' – and they insisted on sketching a map of the United States, in the centre of which they drew a square.

'Iowa? Square?'

Both nodded proudly.

'You'll be going back there soon, I suppose.'

They shrugged and looked back to the simple map, disappointed.

'By Christmas, they reckon.'

'Well, that's something to look forward to.'

The man nodded. The other watched him, looked up to me and signalled that I should not pursue the matter. I understood and began once again to ask them about the fishing. Both began to explain, arguing over the fish they had caught and their individual talents as we drank the beer. Later, the man who had signalled explained that the previous Christmas the other's wife had been killed in a road accident, and that as a consequence he had volunteered to stay behind.

'And you volunteered to stay with him,' I guessed.

He shrugged and shouted to the man who had gone outside.

We stood along the beach, three rods stuck upright in the shingle. I watched their quivering tips as the two men stretched themselves out in the shadow of the dunes.

'What about the fish?' I shouted, surprised by their casual neglect.

'You'll know soon enough,' they shouted back, laughing together at my ignorance and concern.

I joined them in the warm sand as they discussed the prospect of the long walk back to the lorry they had arranged to meet.

Mid afternoon, a line of four aircraft passed above us, their slipstreams becoming scribbled lines which drifted apart and faded. They looked up, identifying the aircraft, their destinations and the likely members of their crews. The planes shone and lost their shape in the sun. Beneath them, the unsettled gulls rose to fill the air with their screams. Behind us, hidden by the dunes, we heard the shouts of the children.

It was only as I referred once again to the return of Mary's father that they began to talk of the war, shaking their heads and interspersing their comments with short silences. They spoke of lost aircrews, friends, of their growing resentment as the daylight missions lost more and more aircraft. When they were unable to continue, they rose to inspect the rods, tugging at the lines and watching them rise from the water. I expressed my disappointment at not having caught anything and they laughed.

Some of the older children climbed to the crest of the dunes and watched us. The men shouted to them, but even the promise of more chocolate or a spell with the rods would not entice them to approach us.

Also watching us, I saw the men, beyond the lighthouse where their boats were beached. I saw Donald Owen and waved. The sergeants turned to look, but the men ignored us.

'British reserve,' the man beside me said sarcastically, drawing out the words and smiling to himself. I wanted to apologise for the men's behaviour.

'They're just a bit unsure, that's all. They're all a bit worried about what's going to happen to them.'

They nodded, only half convinced.

Later, I saw Mary walk alone along the dunes, descending to stand a few yards from us. I invited her to join us, but she shook her head and continued walking.

'Strange kid.'

'She's worried about her father, I suppose.' I resented having to make excuses for her unnecessary rudeness.

'Oh, yeah, her father.'

We caught no fish, but neither of them seemed disappointed, both promising to return as I walked with them to where they had arranged to meet the lorry.

I returned alone, passing the women who had congregated at the road's end. At my approach they lowered their voices and then fell silent. As I passed they nodded politely, causing me to feel immediately and unaccountably guilty, as though I had betrayed them in some way by inviting the Americans.

The lighthouse smelled of tobacco smoke and beer, the empty bottles still standing where we had arranged them around the map of America with its square heart of Iowa still intact.

I met Donald Owen again that same night, passing him on the beach as darkness forced me to abandon my inspection of the fortifications to the south of the Light. These had been erected at the turn of the century purely as a defence against the sea. They were not to be demolished, but already the waves had undercut those nearest the high water line. Beside the defensive wall, two bunkers had been constructed, full now of blown sand and completely hidden from the sea and their intended fields of fire. The structures had become the solid foci around which screes of sand had collected, thick with the grass which camouflaged the concrete outlines even further. The bunkers had been hastily and badly built, remaining only as defences against flood tides, protecting one side of the Light and preventing the sea from flooding the site of the new station. On the landward side of the dunes at this point grew a mass of impenetrable bramble and an occasional gorse bush. Other than the stiff grass, only these two plants seemed capable of surviving under such exposed conditions. Paths through the bushes had been created and maintained by the children, and in places there were signs of recent shallow tunnelling. The gun slits of the bunkers had been sealed, but both structures had been excavated. In five years, the entire defensive line would be completely buried.

In the darkness, invisible birds called from the fields, and a solitary light marked the distant line of houses. On either side of me, the bushes rose to shoulder height before being planed flat by the offshore winds.

In parts, the sea-facing platform of broken concrete rocked as I walked over it. I heard the clatter of disturbed pebbles falling into hollow spaces beneath, and the almost imperceptible noise of shifting sand. The platform needed breaking and dismantling to make it safe, but that would have required too great an extension to our already tight schedule. I knew that the children played there, but knew also that any attempt to warn them or their parents would be gratefully received and then ignored.

Donald Owen stood alone, drawing in a line which he coiled around a wooden spool. At his feet a lantern shone brilliantly over the wet shingle, casting his shadow into the water and picking out the two white bodies which lay beside it.

Hearing me approach, he turned to look, lowering the spool and shouting for me to identify myself.

I stood beside him, pointing to the bank of mist which remained offshore, faintly luminescent in the darkness. He assured me that it would remain where it was for at least another fortnight. I gave him a cigarette which he smoked without removing it from his mouth, winding in his line and warning me of the trailing hooks which rose at regular intervals, many of them still baited with strips of fish. Where these were missing, he swore.

'You'll have nigh on finished the breaking,' he said without turning from the sea.

'The demolition, yes.'

'And then what?'

'The new coastguard station, I suppose.'

He nodded. 'But not you?'

'No, not me.'

Our conversation was interrupted as he began once again to swear and move from side to side in an effort to free his line from where it had become snagged. I helped him, and together we were able to free it.

'I'll have been here fifteen years come autumn,' he announced unexpectedly, apparently unconcerned at the loss of his job and the changes which would force him away. 'They'll put in new boats, I suppose. Proper lifeboats.'

'I suppose so.'

He nodded to himself. 'The old ones were never any good, you know. Never any good in a rising sea. We used to make out that they were, but they weren't.'

'So you're in favour of the new station and new boats?'

'Yes, I suppose I am.' His answer surprised me.

'And the new crews?'

'Yes, them too.'

'You don't sound too upset at what's likely to happen. I thought – '

'No. It's been coming a long time, all this. Besides which, none of the blokes would know the first thing about taking one of the new boats out. They're none of them born sailors.' He laughed.

'And yourself?'

'No, me neither.'

'But what about your homes? Surely – '

'No, not even that. I'm lucky, I suppose, in that I've only got myself to fend for.'

'But some of the others are going to find it hard when the time comes for them to have to leave.' I was thinking of Mary's mother.

'Yes, I suppose they are. Her, you mean.' He turned to look towards the dark outline of the houses.

He was the only one to whom I had spoken who had fully accepted the inevitability of the eviction from Cable Point. I realised also that in never before speaking to him, I had misjudged him, having considered him only in relation to Mary and her mother and his relationship with the woman during her husband's absence.

'They resent my presence,' I said. 'And all this.' I pointed in the direction of the site.

'No, not resent; they're just uncertain of what's happening to them, that's all. Nobody tells them, you see.'

'You don't seem too concerned, though.'

He laughed again. 'No, perhaps not. But as I said, I've got a lot less to lose than any of the others. Besides which, there's nothing here for me, not now.' He knelt to inspect the two fish at his feet, dragging them from the rising tide, lifting them by their gills to guess their weight. 'He'll be back on Friday,' he said unexpectedly, his back to me.

'Yes, I know.'

'I can't see as things are going to be very easy for him – not with all this going on. They hadn't even put the guns in when he left.' By 'they' he meant me.

'No, I don't suppose it is.'

'You know about him, I suppose – about what happened to him?'

'Spending the war as a prisoner, you mean?'

He nodded, and I sensed that he wanted to tell me more.

After a further silence, I said, 'Mary told me about the body.'

'Body?'

'The German sailor who was washed up.'

'German? It wasn't no German; just a lad from a coaster sunk up off Grimsby. He washed up four days after. They came to collect him. It was the kids that found him.'

'But Mary told me you'd told her he was a German sailor.'

'She told you that?'

I nodded.

'No, he wasn't no German.'

'I'm sorry, she – '

He shook his head, and I tried to remember what else she had told me, about the body being naked.

'She told you about me and her mother, I suppose.'

I was uncertain of what to say, of how much I had guessed or been told.

'It doesn't matter now, I don't suppose. At one time we might have, well . . . But that was two years ago, two years after she'd first heard about him. I suppose she never really thought he'd be coming back. I don't suppose either of us did.'

'No, I suppose not.'

He laughed coldly. 'And it's not the best place in the world for keeping a secret, especially one like that.'

'And it was all over two years ago?'

'Yes. Why, did you think we were still – ?'

'No, I – it's – '

'Mary tell you that as well, did she?'

'I'm not sure; she might have implied . . .'

'I'm sure she probably did,' he said, turning back to his line.

I told him of how her young brother had mistaken me for their father. He listened carefully to the details, genuinely concerned at the implications. We watched the water for the splashing fight of another fish.

'You and he didn't get on very well together?' I guessed.

He shook his head. 'No, nor did they, him and her. When his call-up came he jumped at it. After the birth of the youngest he couldn't – ' He stopped and shook his head. 'It hardly seems right to be telling you all this.'

'No, of course not. I'm sorry.'

He knelt to shake free a small flatfish, vividly white in the darkness, no bigger than his palm, curling as it flexed, suspended in mid-air. He picked it from where it fell and threw it back into the water.

'Will you still be here when he gets back?'

I said I would.

'It means a lot to her this, you know.'

I said 'Yes,' but was uncertain of what he meant.

I left him and watched from the dunes as he continued to reel in his lines, the same motions over and over in the glow of the lamp.

eight

'Of course, I knew Michael personally,' the padre said defensively, sharing a glance with the man beside him, as though expecting me to challenge him for proof of what he said. His words embarrassed the captain, who took a large brown envelope from his briefcase and held it in his lap, waiting for my attention. The padre continued speaking, but my attention was claimed by the envelope which the captain began to tap, like a conductor calling for silence. He seemed nervous, thinking of how to begin what he had to say.

On one sheet I read the two dates of my son's injury and death. I read them aloud, realising for the first time how short a period it had really been. At the sound of my voice the padre stopped speaking, surprised, uncertain.

'We all understand how, er, difficult it must be for you to, er, come to terms with your son's death, especially under circumstances such as – '

'No, not really.' My thoughts had become words. I stopped, surprised by my ability to confess them to these strangers.

The padre smiled nervously, about to say something religious and comforting in which he no longer believed. The captain lied and said that he understood.

The padre said, 'Oh, yes, I see,' and then fell silent, his unnecessary platitude embarrassing us all.

After a further silence, I said, 'You said you knew Michael personally. Had you seen him recently?'

'Recently?'

'In Ireland.'

'No, sorry. I'm afraid I only knew him before he was posted.'

'I see.'

'Sorry.'

The captain watched us impatiently, waiting for the chance to speak. Straightening the papers in his lap, he began to present the forms it would be necessary for me to sign in order for Michael's body to be released. He spoke quickly, using the forms and procedures to distance himself from the darker side of his task.

'He was a fine soldier,' the padre said uselessly, stopping abruptly as both I and the captain turned to face him. I thanked him, wanting to both believe and reassure him. The captain turned back to me. Perhaps he wanted to tell me that Michael had been careless, that he had risked the lives of others, that he had made the kind of mistake no good soldier would make. I waited for him to speak, but he did not – partly, I knew, because of the man beside him, and partly because he was still uncertain of my own feelings.

It was the absence on my part of any outward show of grief which confused them. Perhaps if they had dealt with his mother they would have felt more comfortable, more assured of the need for what they were there to do. It struck me, sitting in that warm room, discussing the return of my son's body, that he could have been the son of any one of us; that anyone watching who did not understand what was happening would have been unable – except for the uniforms – to distinguish between us.

I asked if they anticipated any delays.

'Delays?' The padre looked to the captain, who shook his head, relieved that we had at last arrived at the practicalities of the situation.

'Have you been given details of the arrival and arrangements for transfer to a civilian undertaker?'

I said that I had.

'Good. No – no delays. This kind of thing is usually surprisingly straightforward. We try to ensure that everything is dealt with as smoothly as possible in order to enable you to . . .'

I nodded to let him know I understood, wondering how many other parents there had been.

'Your wife,' the padre said. 'How is – I mean is she – ?'

'I'm afraid my wife is taking this much more badly than I am.'

'Ah, yes, of course.' He seemed relieved that at least one of us had sufficient decency or sense to have responded according to the demands of the situation.

'Is she – ?'

'Upstairs.'

'Should I – ?'

'I don't think it would help. She went to see him, you see. When he was injured she went across to visit him.'

'Ah, yes, of course.' He had clearly not known, and once again his silence embarrassed us all.

The interview was concluded with the fanning out of yet more forms and pamphlets on the low table. At the door, the captain turned and thanked me. 'It's never easy,' he said. 'But sometimes . . .' I told him I understood, and in his handshake I felt his relief that the meeting was over.

It was only later, as I sat alone, that I realised how I must have seemed to them. They would misinterpret my apparent coldness and then perhaps they would wish that all fathers were the same.

She came down several hours later, as the heat of the day and the evening's coolness began to balance each other out. She made no attempt to question me about their visit, but simply closed the french windows and sat opposite me in the fading light. There were red lines across her cheek where she

had fallen asleep on the bed. She had been crying and her
eyes were dark.

In 1953, the storms and high tides which breached and
flooded the East Coast destroyed what remained of the fringe
of seaward fortifications around the new coastguard station
at Cable Point. Neither the station nor the lighthouse suffered any structural harm, but the exposed terrace of houses,
already having stood empty for five years, was damaged to the
extent that they had to be demolished. On the landward side
of the dunes, fields as far as fifteen miles inland were flooded
as the drains surged and burst. The road to Cable Point was
broken in several places and afterwards rebuilt. Work on the
new living accommodation was delayed, although the foundations and rising walls remained comparatively undamaged.

Less than a mile offshore, two small freighters were sunk
within a hundred yards of each other and seven lives were lost.
A further nine men were rescued by the new lifeboat. A year
following the storms, a plaque was set into the base of the
coastguard station commemorating the action, and the boat
stationed there was renamed after one of the sunken freighters.

In November of 1955 I returned to Cable Point for the first
time in eight years. At the time I was working in Belgium,
home for only a month. Michael, I remember, celebrated his
fourth birthday whilst I was there.

New fortifications had been erected on the site of those I
had previously built and then destroyed. The lighthouse stood
taller and whiter than I had remembered it, its wooden door
replaced by a metal one. The sand-covered wasteland between
the tower and the new station had been cleared and asphalted
over. The brambles and warren of bunkers to the south were
all that remained.

As I left my car to climb the dunes, two Alsatians emerged,
barking excitedly and jumping at the wire mesh of their
compound. A uniformed man appeared in the doorway of the
station and watched me through binoculars.

The dunes, too, had been reinforced, planted with girders

and lined with sack-shaped blocks of concrete tipped at random from above the high water line. The steep bank of shingle remained, still with its tidal collars of discarded rope, weed and feathers. The gulls, too, seemed to be present in even greater numbers, hanging above me in the wind.

All that remained of the houses were their infilled foundations, the lines of their dividing walls still discernible, and black stains where their hearths had been. In the once barren gardens grew almost perfect squares of nettles. The new road was raised and lined with white bollards, and I remembered the women's useless efforts at keeping it clear of sand after each day's wind.

Walking onto the plot where Mary's home had stood, I was unable to believe how small the site actually was.

Nothing remained of the fortifications opposite the houses: the acres of uneven ground were now perfectly flat, fenced, paved and spotlighted with brilliant white lights which cut through the falling darkness of that November afternoon.

Only on the open land beyond the perimeter of the station did the unevenness of the ground betray where debris still lay buried in a narrow band between the new buildings and the first of the adjoining fields.

A formation of three perfectly spaced jets passed overhead, and the dogs resumed their barking at the delayed roar. There were no trails against the grey sky, only circles of flame as the planes continued low over the ground in the direction of Lincoln.

The man with the binoculars was still watching me as I returned to my car and left.

At the point where the road turned along the coast stood a line of weatherboard chalets which, judging by their condition, must have been erected soon after my departure in 1946. Beside them stood several blue- and cream-coloured caravans with porches of flimsy trelliswork. Sand blew across what might once have been tended gardens, and on the land in front of those chalets still inhabited ran uneven lines of white and whitewashed pebbles. A wreath of smoke curled from one chimney, and the silent, watching gulls crowded across the curved roofs of the caravans.

The line of dilapidated homes seemed aware of its own impermanence, and of its rapid decay in the face of the sea and wind. Some of the buildings were named – black and gold lettering on slices of varnished wood swinging on short chains. Each of the structures appeared to have been continually repainted, layers of colour peeling to reveal bleached grey wood beneath.

A woman stood at the window of one of the chalets and watched as I drove past. She lifted the sheet of net curtain and looked from the road to the waiting gulls, vividly white against the dark sky.

I parked beyond the bend and looked back. The rain had stopped and the wipers moved in wasted actions across the windscreen. Opening the door, I listened to the pounding of the sea as it scraped at the shingle.

part two

one

The war, it seemed, clung to everything, too long and powerful to leave no frayed edges, no ineradicable stains, no men fighting in its wake. To everything, that is, except the newspapers, where it was no longer profitable, and where to forget it seemed the best policy. It clung to me and to the dark wainscoted walls of the courtroom in which I had come to give my testimony.

Would I really be able to stand before them and honestly admit that I had no idea, no premonition of what was to happen at Cable Point? I waited alone, listening to each sound in the corridor outside, expecting at any moment to see the others as they, too, almost eighteen months later, prepared their own versions of what had happened.

The winter of 1947–8 was particularly harsh, and my journey had been uncomfortably long and uncertain. The silent room gave me time to gather my thoughts. In the corridor I heard voices and then footsteps. Names were called, repeated at intervals as if in echo, and occasionally there were sudden expectant silences during which individual words and pronouncements might be heard.

There was a single high window in the room, from which I gained only an impression of the colour of the sky. There was no sun, and later there would be snow heavy enough to threaten my return journey. The door opened and closed without anyone entering. In the corridor, two men shared a joke and laughed. I folded my newspaper and coughed loudly, embarrassed by the room's silence and my presence within it, as though, despite having been directed, I shouldn't have been there.

The thought that any of the others might arrive only added to my discomfort.

I was watching the window when the door opened for a second time. A man entered and read my name from a sheet of paper. He apologised for having kept me waiting, smiled and held the door as I followed him out and into the Court.

Afterwards, I did see two of the women with their husbands. They approached me and we exchanged formal greetings. They had already left Cable Point, and after nervously commenting on the tribunal, the women began to talk about their new homes. But their excited descriptions seemed forced solely for my benefit, concerned too much with what they thought they had gained rather than what they had lost. The men stood silently behind, shaking and nodding their heads at everything their wives said. They had been dispossessed, and they spoke of the place as though it was somewhere alien to them, somewhere they too had only read about in the newspapers in connection with what had happened there.

He was expected to arrive at four in the afternoon. For that reason I suggested to the men that they waive their right to remain on the beach and that they return to Lincoln early. It was Friday, and with the prospect of a long weekend ahead of them, few objected.

From midday onwards, his wife continually appeared in the doorway, searching the pale road as if for a tell-tale signal of dust, and scanning the indistinct horizon for sign of his return. She looked over spaces ten miles distant, where the expanse of open fields was reduced to lines, and where the occasional flash of sunlight indicated a moving car.

The children, too, were more subdued than usual, gathering in a group beside the road and walking towards where it curved and disappeared, returning disappointed as four o'clock arrived and passed.

On the inland horizon, cones of black smoke rose from burning fields, reminding me of the pulsing smoke of oil and rubber, blossoming like ink spilled in water, its shadow over running men as they threw sand and shouted names on the edge of a desert; beside them lay a row of bodies, sheeted and sand-covered, and looking already like temporary, unmarked graves. As unexpectedly as it had arrived, the memory ended and I looked back to the waiting woman.

She remained apart from the others, Mary beside her, holding her hand. Earlier, I had seen them together on the beach. And later, as the lorries left, I saw them walk along the narrow path which separated the site from the surrounding fields. I made no effort to join them, and they in turn appeared oblivious to my presence as they returned through the piles of rubble and draped machinery.

At five he had still not arrived. The other women stood outside, openly discussing the delay, as though they too had been let down. I wanted them to leave, to allow the woman to wait alone. It was only when they did finally disperse that Mary and her mother emerged to stand beside the roadway. Mary's dress had been washed and ironed, and her mother wore a tight-fitting cardigan over a blue blouse and skirt. Her loose hair had been tied into a bun, making her look younger. She continually rubbed her arms, although the sun had not yet begun to lose its heat. Mary held a white handkerchief, as though either expecting to cry or to cheer like the countless cheering children of the cinema newsreels.

As I watched, her mother turned to face her, smoothing creases from her dress, smiling at something she said.

The remainder of the children waited on the opposite side of the road, climbing the blocks and pointing to the distance where they saw everything and nothing. The other women remained indoors – either out of respect for the reunion or to hide their own uncertainties, preferring to observe rather than become involved. Occasionally, a face would appear, a cheek pressed to the glass. The woman remained oblivious to the glances, but Mary turned and returned the stares until the faces withdrew. I closed the lighthouse door, watching unobserved from the second floor window. From where I stood I was able to see the road along its entire length, and would be the first to witness the man's arrival.

Above the silence rose the intermittent noise of a wireless set, the cries of the gulls, and the shouts of the younger children, impatient for something to happen. At each sound the woman turned, first in the direction from which it had come, and then back to the road ahead of her.

At seven, the van arrived, stopping short of the road's end. A man emerged and stood beside it. He shouted into the cab and pointed to the houses. It was a military vehicle, khaki-coloured with white stencilled lettering, moving slowly forward to the road's end, its heavy tyres dipping forward into the soft sand. The man approached the waiting women, unfolding a sheet of paper which he presented to them. The driver remained in the cab, smoking. From the woman's anxious glances and the hand held to her face, I knew that neither of the men was her husband. I imagined then that a terrible mistake had been made and that they had come to tell her that her husband would not be coming home – a case of mistaken identity – and that somewhere else there was another woman, another wife and mother waiting in precisely the same way for the return of a husband she had long believed dead.

I heard the man's voice as he read from the paper, pointing for her to see and laughing loudly at something he had said.

On the opposite side of the road, the children formed into a line, moving cautiously forward to the edge of the broken ground. The man in the cab saw them and shouted. They stopped, ducking instinctively. He shouted again before jumping stiffly down, arching and rubbing his back. He walked to the rear of the van and held open its doors, speaking to someone inside. The children rose and grouped together. The man with the women held open the gate, but neither Mary nor her mother followed him out onto the road. From the rear of the van a third man appeared, holding a folded blanket which the driver took from him, supporting his arm as he stepped down onto the road. Mary held her mother's arm and led her towards him. The precise moment of their reunion was hidden from me by the van.

The driver and his mate moved to stand beside the children, asking them questions about the lighthouse and the expanse of broken land beyond. A door opened and a woman stepped out to shake a cloth. Mary reappeared and walked back to the open gate. Her mother and father followed, the man shielding his eyes to look around him before being helped indoors.

two

During his first tour, he wrote regularly, using the same careful words and phrases, balancing news of his friends and what he was doing with constant references to home, to what she and he had discussed. She wrote back, and his letters became filled with reminiscences, reliving the past at the expense of being able to share with us what was happening to him there and then. Perhaps he preferred it that way. Perhaps that is what he was encouraged to do. The letters revived her memories, and she, too, began to retreat, measuring what we had become against what we had been in his presence. It would serve no purpose for me to dispute anything he said.

She constantly re-read the letters and wrote at length about the irrelevant minutiae of what was happening around her. She wrote about the garden, about our increasingly fewer social engagements and about the people whom she had seen and who had asked after him. They always asked and she told them at length of the things about which he had written. They asked out of politeness and then nodded politely as she told them, becoming embarrassed and uncertain of her eagerness to talk. She, of course, saw nothing of this, and on the few occasions when I had suggested that people didn't want to hear every detail, she would smile and ask them if she was boring them. They, of course, would deny it, and in this way she claimed her small victories.

I wrote less frequently, frustrated by her censorship and by the things I found myself unable to express.

He wrote twice a month, but every morning she searched the mail, saving his letters to read alone, making no attempt to disguise the fact from me, propping them conspicuously upon the mantelpiece to await my return. And as I read them she would repeat what he had written, adding opinions of her own or waiting for my confirmations and reassurances. In many letters he repeated himself simply because of his difficulty in perpetuating the falsehoods she needed to hear. She, of course, saw none of this; or if she did she chose to ignore it. As I read I wondered if he had thought of me, of what I would think and believe. He must certainly have known that my own understanding of what was happening to him would be greater than hers, and I took comfort in the realisation that the letters were written for her alone, knowing that between him and me there must remain an unwritten understanding. In this way I felt closer to him than I ever had done before.

During his absences she began spending increasingly longer periods without leaving the house or garden, venturing no further – not even to pursue the reassuring routines upon which she now depends in coming to terms with his death.

On several occasions she accused the newspaper reports of being inaccurate or even deliberately misleading, as if she could in some way protect him by protecting herself. Once, upon hearing of the deaths of two other soldiers, she had laughed with relief, reassuring herself with the remark that her son would never be so careless, as if a daily quota of deaths had been filled and he had remained unhurt. I shouted at her and told her not to be so stupid, so insensitive and blind to what was happening to him. I expected her to argue, but instead she became immediately calm and accused me of having no feelings. I chose not to prolong the argument, and she took comfort in what she mistakenly believed to be her own inner strength.

Sometimes the letters would arrive when I was away. These, I later discovered, she had not shown me, but had kept hidden in her dressing-table, re-reading and sharing their secrets in my absence. In some letters there were more photographs, mostly badly taken, which she began to arrange throughout the house, several in every room.

There is a picture of him with one of his friends, neither of them in uniform, laughing, eyes closed, their arms across the shoulders of two girls. She wanted to know if I thought they were local. Believing they were worried her. I said that I thought it unlikely. In another photograph he is standing beside a painted wall, in uniform, his face smudged black, an upright rifle cradled in the fold of his arm. Around him stand a group of small children, all staring at the camera, their faces betraying no emotion other than the excitement of having their picture taken. He, too, is smiling. I have seen the same picture, other sons, a thousand times. There is something disturbing about it, something in the way he looks and the way in which the children crowd so close. Perhaps there is a measure of protection in having them so near. They appear unconcerned by his presence, the camera a greater novelty than his gun.

She is reassured by the picture, pointing to the children, expressing her sympathy for them and the environment in which they are growing. I agree with her, but for different reasons.

The day following his arrival, neither he nor his wife left their home. I saw Mary mid morning and asked her how he was. 'Why?' she asked defensively, turning away but hesitating sufficiently to suggest that I should persist. She had, I guessed, been told to leave the house, and from where we sat at the start of the dunes she turned continually to look towards the closed door and drawn curtains.

'The man said he'll have to go back to hospital in Lincoln. They're sending another van to pick him up.'

'For long?'

She shook her head. 'Just for a day. It's like you said.'

'Like I said?'

She nodded but made no attempt to explain.

'I daresay they'll keep an eye on him for some time. Until he's fully recovered, I shouldn't think – '

'He's thin,' she said suddenly. 'His arms are . . .' She held out her own and looked at them.

'He's been very ill, don't forget,' I said, watching her.

'And when he walks he's so slow.' She kicked her bare feet into the sand, watching as the depressions filled. 'In the letter the man said he'd made a good recovery, and the man with the van said that it was better for him to be at home than in a hospital in London. He said that he – ' she stopped and dug her hands into the brittle grass beside her. Clearly, she was upset and angry – both at the condition in which her father had returned and at her own unfulfilled expectations. She was frustrated also at being unable to express her disappointment in a way in which it might make sense. She felt cheated, but was uncertain of how to respond to what had happened.

'You'll need to give him more time to settle back into the routine of things. He's been away a long time and things have changed a lot since – '

'All this, you mean?' She pointed towards the site.

'Yes, this. And other things. You can't expect him to come back exactly as he went away.' I hoped that by expressing what she found so difficult to admit to, I might make things easier for her, or that by saying these things she would at least realise that I understood.

'Will he ever be like he was?'

'I don't know. I suppose that depends on how he manages to readjust and on what the doctors in Lincoln decide.'

'But they told us he was all right – that he'd been ill but that he'd made a good recovery. That's what they said – a good recovery.'

All along, both she and her mother had been told too little upon which to base their expectations; and what they had been told had been conveniently ambiguous, designed to raise their spirits rather than to prepare them for the practical realities of what his return would mean. This was why she felt

cheated. She had been encouraged by what she now saw as lies.
Her mother's disappointment must have been equally great.

'What about your mother?'

She shrugged, seemingly unconcerned, and said simply,
'She wore that skirt when he went off.'

'The one she wore last night?'

'Yes. She said he'd be glad to see her in it, but he never said
a word.' She paused and turned to face me. 'Were you
watching us, then?'

'I saw the van arrive, yes.' I expected her to be angry, but
instead she smiled, scooping up a handful of sand and watching
as it trickled through her fingers onto her legs.

'They were all watching, you know. None of them came
out, but they were all watching.'

'I suppose it's only natural that they should take an interest.'

'She didn't see them, but I knew they were there.' I
wondered why she insisted on repeating the point. 'The man in
the van said that she could go with him to Lincoln if she
wanted.'

'And will she?'

She shook her head. 'She said I could go instead. They're
sending his stuff up on a train and we've got to go to the
station and collect it.'

'Well, if you let me know when it's due, then perhaps I
could arrange for one of the lorries to pick it up.'

'That's what she said.'

'Yes, well . . .'

She stood up and pointed again over the site. 'Where is
everybody?'

'Saturday, remember?'

'Are they coming back on Monday?'

'Yes, of course. Why?'

'Oh, nothing.' I wanted to insist on an answer, but she
began to climb the slope behind us. From the top she looked
down to where I sat. 'The man said that perhaps there was a
place in Lincoln where he could work.'

'A job? That's good.' I followed her up the slope.

'No, not a proper job; he said it was a "re-" something.'

'A re-training centre?'

'That's it – re-training.' She repeated the word to herself. 'He said there were lots of them.'

'Yes, there are. It sounds like a good idea. And will he go?' She shrugged.

'Well perhaps the doctors in Lincoln will sort something out for him.'

She stopped ahead of me and turned. 'There's nothing wrong with him, you know! He is all right!'

'Yes, I – '

'He isn't funny or anything. He's not – ' She jabbed at her forehead, shouting, unsure of what it was she was defending, of her own feelings about her father's condition.

'No, of course not.' I took out my cigarettes and she asked if I would give her one to take to him. I gave her the packet and she counted them, smiling at the thought of being able to present them to him.

'You'd better take these, too.' I threw her the box of matches. It was an unnecessary gesture, but one I needed to make.

She came towards me and brushed at the ash which had fallen onto my chest. 'He's got a uniform and things with the rest of his stuff,' she said, touching the button of my pocket. I wanted to say something and to remove her hand. 'The man with the van said he'd got a medal.'

'Your father – dad?'

She nodded proudly. 'He hasn't got it yet, though. They gave her some forms about getting his money and things like that. He said there were lots of them, all coming out of hospital and going home. Do you think he was telling the truth?'

'I don't see why not.' My answer disappointed her and she withdrew her hand.

'I've got to go now.' She touched the cigarettes through the material of her dress.

I watched as she descended the slope and crossed the road

to the houses. Several of the women shouted to her, hoping to engage her in conversation. One of them gave her a white jug and a newspaper-wrapped parcel, following her to the door. Another of them saw me and waved. I waved back and they came towards me.

It was not until three days after his return that I first met the man.

On Monday I had avoided using the power drills and noisier pieces of machinery. Consequently, our time had been spent in clearing those parts of the site already demolished, removing the rubble to expose the maze of foundations and underground corridors. The work was relatively easy, and the men seemed in better spirits than they had been during the previous weeks.

On that third evening I paced the outline of the new station, making a note of those foundations yet to be levelled and those to be filled in. I stood with my back to the houses, checking the plans and drawing imaginary lines over the ground.

Mary was the first to leave the house, followed by her father. She waited at the road, signalling him to follow her. I wondered if she had seen me in the fading light as they moved slowly towards where I stood. She saw me and waved, continuing to point things out to him, and to warn him of where the slabs were unsafe as he moved cautiously over them.

She introduced us and I held out my hand. He instinctively moved his own behind his back and looked to her.

'This is my dad,' she announced proudly. 'I was showing him where all the buildings have been.'

'Feel free,' I said, seeing the man's nervous reaction to her words, as though perhaps he believed they were trespassing.

I offered him a cigarette and he smiled, releasing her arm and wiping his palms down the front of his shirt before accepting.

'You sent me the others,' he said. 'Very grateful. I – they didn't – didn't – ' He began to shake. Mary touched him and he stopped immediately, smiling at me and holding the cigarette to his mouth, where it continued to register his movement. He laughed awkwardly and apologised as I held his cupped hands steady to the match.

Heavily tanned, his skin remained unnaturally taut and shiny, transparent almost across his cheeks and forehead, where it stretched and slackened as he spoke. His arm muscles, though wasted, were prominent against the thinness of his limbs. As he spoke he continually closed his eyes, as though the simple effort of keeping them open was too great. This, I realised, was probably the result of whatever medication he might still be receiving. I knew him to be in his mid-thirties, but seeing him like that he might have been twenty years older.

His dark colouring was made even more noticeable by the unnatural whiteness of the false teeth he wore. These, he explained, were new and caused his gums to bleed. He touched them as he spoke, holding out his finger as proof. Beside him, Mary nodded. His own teeth, he told me, had been lost as the result of a disease, the name of which he had never known. Mary nodded again and he smiled down at her, resting an arm across her shoulders. He described the disease and asked me if I might know its name. Mary insisted that I would, and for her sake more than his I suggested a few names. He shook his head at each, laughing coldly at his familiarity with some, his eyes half open and closing.

'She reckons I'll be up and about in a fortnight,' he said, pulling his daughter to him and pushing her hair over her face. She complained and smoothed it back. It did not occur to me then, but in his presence she had become a child again – the child she had been at his departure and the child he had expected upon his return.

'She was showing me where the buildings had been. It's – I – I – ' Once again he began to shake uncontrollably, his eyes closed. I looked at Mary, but she simply shook her head and held his arm. In his mouth the cigarette rose and fell, and after a few seconds the movement subsided. Once again he apologised. I insisted that there was no need. He appeared more embarrassed at having been seen than by whatever the intermittent and uncontrollable spasms might have meant.

'The doctor said that in six months it'll – it'll have passed. It used to be much – '

'It used to be a hundred times worse,' Mary interrupted.

He laughed at her defensive gesture. 'Aye, a hundred times worse at least.'

She nodded vigorously, smiling, holding his hand over her chest.

'She says you've been here all summer.'

'Yes, but another month should just about see us finished.'

'It's ch – changed a good bit since I last – last – ' He shook his head and swore.

'Yes, I daresay. Thankfully it won't always be as unsightly as this.' I stopped, realising that he was unlikely to be there long enough to see any of the improvements. Mary turned to me, her eyes narrowed, angry that I had anticipated what he had been trying to say, that I had said it for him. Now my presence seemed to make her uneasy, as though I was somehow compelling her to make comparisons between us, and then between what she had expected and what he had become. In the silence which followed he ran his free hand over his face, as though pushing away an insect that had landed there.

'You couldn't even walk at one time, could you, dad?' The question was designed to suggest the improvements already made and the ease with which a complete recovery might be achieved. Of the three of us, I suspect only she believed in what she was suggesting.

'No, love, couldn't barely put one foot in front of the other at one time.'

She nodded, and unseen by her he winked at me.

I pinched the stub of my cigarette and threw it to the ground. He looked down to where it landed, staring at the inch of white as though about to say something. She, too, watched the glowing stub and I realised the mistake I had made, the gulf I had emphasised between us.

'Look, if it's cigarettes you're short of, come up to the lighthouse. I've more than enough for my own needs. You're more than welcome.'

He protested that he couldn't, but I saw from his eyes that he needed to accept. I lied and told him that I smoked them simply because they were there. 'Send Mary up,' I suggested, realising that this was more likely to achieve both our aims. He nodded.

'We've got to go back now,' she announced, taking hold of his wrist. 'We've got this list, and he's not supposed to tire himself out. That's what it says.'

'Naah,' he protested, sounding exactly like the men on the site. 'First time I've been out today. I've spent nine – nine months in a bloody bed and I – I – I – ' He began to shake. This time the spasm lasted a full minute. Instead of holding him as she had done previously, Mary released her grip and moved away. He waved his arm towards her, like a blind man testing for an obstacle. This, I realised, was her way of rein- forcing what she had suggested, of making it clear to us both that she was right and we were wrong.

'S – sorry, mate. It's – I – ' But she was already pulling him away, and I walked with them towards the houses. He spoke again, this time perfectly coherently for several minutes, joking about his daughter's dominant nature. At the gate I insisted again that he take some of the cigarettes. Hearing our voices, his wife came out, watching us apprehensively and smiling as he turned to her.

'Oh, I thought – '

'Thought what?' he shouted to her. 'Thought I'd gone and fallen into one of them bloody holes and had to be carried back?' He laughed cruelly at the suggestion and she watched him uncertainly, glancing from her daughter to me. Mary left him to stand beside her. From inside the house I heard the crying of the small boy.

'We appreciate what you did – the hammers and drills, I mean,' she said, nodding over my shoulder.

'Yes,' he said, looking down, as though ashamed at his

outburst. 'I – ' He stopped and shook his head, uncertain of the pain a memory might cause him.

'Rest, they said. Convalescence.' She, too, seemed uncertain of what she was saying, or why.

He stood beside me and whispered the words as she said them. I thought he was going to make another disparaging remark, but instead he asked for Mary to hold his hand. The woman watched, and he held up his daughter's arm as though intending the simple gesture to hurt them both.

three

'We understand Michael's mother – your wife – we understand . . .' He lifted the sheet of paper and read her full name, waiting for my unnecessary nod of confirmation before continuing. 'We understand she went to see your son in hospital, in Ireland.'

'I already told you that she had.'

'Ah, yes, of course. Sorry. Arrived on the twenty-first.' He waited for another nod, scoring a short line across the sheet and smiling as though he had accomplished something without my knowledge. Beside him, the padre repeated the date and nodded, as though for him, too, it held some greater significance.

'Was there any specific reason for the visit that you know of? Any particular purpose?'

I wanted to shout at him, but she was upstairs, and would have heard. Then she might have come down and been forced, like myself, to endure the embarrassed and embarrassing sympathies with which they filled the gaps between their questions. He saw I was not prepared to answer.

'It was most irregular,' he said defensively.

'So I believe.'

He felt my irritation and drew another line. 'Yes, well . . . according to our records, she arrived on the twenty-first and left three days later on the – '

'Twenty-fourth. Does it really matter?' I became anxious that her visit might have complicated matters, that it might delay his return. It was their second visit.

'No, no, of course not. Naturally, we will do everything within our, er . . .' He began once again to read from the form. 'Ah yes! Did either of you – you or your wife – visit your son at any other time during his active service abroad?'

'No, of course not.'

'Mm. And did your son write to you regularly whilst stationed in Ireland.'

'Yes.'

'How regularly?' I told him about the letters and he understood. He read the contents of a final sheet, passed it to the padre, and clapped the file shut. The padre rose and went to look over the garden.

'Was it ever your wife's intention to bring your son's body back with her?'

The question caught me off guard: I was watching the padre, listening to him as he spoke about his own garden. Perhaps his words were intended to lull me.

The question was repeated.

I turned to the captain, swore at him and then apologised. 'No, of course not!'

'You seem very sure of that.' He smiled smugly.

'When my wife went to see Michael he was injured and unconscious. He died on the thirtieth.'

'Oh, I – I'm sorry, I – ' He began to search for another sheet of paper, as if to convince me that the insensitive mistake had not been his fault.

'Alive?' the padre said, turning from the garden, only half understanding what had happened. Both men apologised. I did the same for having shouted and the padre resumed what he had been saying about the garden. The captain watched him with a look of undisguised irritation, almost contempt. He then pointed to the portrait of my father above the fireplace and said 'Father?' I told him that it was, but refused to provide him with the details of military history he had hoped for.

'A fine man,' he said. 'Someone to be proud of.' Implying, I thought, that he had known him.

'You think so?' I wondered again how many other homes he and the padre had visited with their tragic double act. Perhaps they wanted me to be proud of my son's sacrifice.

'He will be returned in full dress uniform, of course.'

'What? Sorry, I wasn't . . .'

'Full dress uniform.'

'Yes, of course. Thank you.' I felt suddenly defeated. What did it matter how he was returned? Perhaps if the padre had not been present and I had been completely devoid of feeling, I would have asked about his amputated feet.

The captain continued to look at the framed photograph of my father, as though there might be some quality in the face or erect body via which he might understand me.

'Grief affects people in many ways,' the padre repeated uselessly in my defence, still not turning from the garden.

A few small clouds moved across the sky, their shadows a running blemish on the calm sea, as though a school of whales was moving slowly beneath its surface.

'You've seen him, then?' Donald Owen nodded in answer to his own question. We sat together, away from the houses and in the cool, elongated shadow of the Light.

'Yes, a couple of days ago.'

'And since?'

'No – only at a distance, usually with Mary.'

He nodded, clasping his knees and leaning forward to re-arrange the spools of line at his feet.

'Has he changed much?' I asked. I knew from the photographs I had seen that outwardly at least his appearance had altered dramatically.

'It's funny, that,' he said. 'Because for all the obvious differences, he's still the same bloke underneath. He always had this – this unpredictable streak, I suppose you'd call it. Mean, too, when he wanted to be.'

'Violent, you mean?'

'On occasion. It's funny, but whenever anybody was about he could be the nicest bloke in the world – nice to her, to the kids . . .' He hesitated, unsure of how much he should tell me.

'But?'

'I don't know – perhaps it's not right to talk about him like this – not after . . .'

I agreed with him, putting him at ease by indicating that I, too, had detected something calculating in the man's behaviour, something beneath all his nervous and physical disabilities which left me uncertain and uneasy.

'Yes, calculating, that's it. Nice as pie when he wanted to be. But when it was just him and her, or the kids . . .' He raised his arms in a gesture I understood.

'Perhaps it's no longer there,' I said unconvincingly. 'Perhaps it's been forced out of him, or whatever.'

'Perhaps.'

'I doubt if any of this is going to help matters,' I said, indicating the demolition site, expressing the same fears I had shared with his wife.

He shook his head. 'I shouldn't worry too much about that: he was never cut out for all this – not living right out here, like this, with her and the kids. He only came here in the first place because the house went with the job. I don't think either of them really knew what they were letting themselves in for.'

'Perhaps he's still suffering from the after-effects of whatever treatment they've been giving him,' I suggested.

'Perhaps you're right. But it's still there. We can't ignore it – not in a place like this, not with all this happening.'

'No, I suppose not.' But I remained unconvinced of our ability or even our intentions of doing anything positive to either help the man or relieve the situation.

'It's as if everything else has been knocked out of him or peeled away. As if this was the hardest part of him, the one thing they couldn't touch.' He laughed to avoid any further explanation of what he was trying to say. I told him I thought I understood what he meant.

'Oh, it's there all right. It's there.'

'But surely he won't be capable of any violence – of any physical violence now: he seems too weak, too dependent on others, too – '

'Yes, perhaps you're right.' He spoke to stop me, and I sensed that he wanted the conversation to end, that he knew or suspected something he did not want me to arrive at.

I realised then how frustrating it must have been to be a violent man inside a body incapable of even the least exertion – of being betrayed by a physical weakness from which there was little chance of recovery.

'Were things bad before his call-up?'

'Sometimes. In the months before his departure things eased up a bit. But before that . . .'

'Mary never said anything about him – about that side of him, I mean.'

'Oh?' He seemed surprised and spoke quickly to hide his feelings. 'No, well, I don't suppose kids really understand what's happening. Perhaps they only remember what they want to.'

'I always thought she was his favourite.'

He nodded and turned back to his lines, reluctant to continue, repeating the word 'favourite' to himself.

I apologised, saying it was none of my business. He shook his head and said something I did not hear, but which I knew not to ask him to repeat.

After a silence in which we smoked and waited for the rising tide, he said, 'It'll take some time yet, I suppose, his recovery.'

'Yes, I daresay. Although I suspect it's mostly up to him now – to how he responds to coming home, to the treatment in Lincoln, and to what happens to him from here onwards.'

'You don't think there'll be a job for him on the new station, then?'

'I doubt it. Mary said something about a re-training centre.'

He laughed. 'He'll not stick that, not in a thousand years.'

I considered my next question carefully, prepared for the consequences. 'Does his presence here worry you?'

125

'Because of me and her, you mean?'

I nodded.

'Does it show?'

'Sometimes.'

'No, not really – not for my own sake, anyway.'

'For her, then?'

He nodded reluctantly. 'I know it's stupid – him being how he is and everything – but I can't help feeling that there's something we've all missed, something even the doctors have overlooked.'

'Such as?'

But he shook his head and began to untangle a knot of line and hooks.

'But you still think he's capable of violence – of mistreating them?'

He nodded, and beneath us the shingle started to slide as the tide rose through it. On the horizon, the low bank of mist obscured the divide between sea and sky. In the shadow of the Light, it remained cool, and we were free of the flies which swarmed over the rest of the beach. Occasionally, he slapped his cheek or forehead, leaving stains where they had died. He told me that it kept off the others.

'Perhaps it's just as well that part of his old self has endured,' I said. 'Perhaps it's enough for him to build from and recover. Perhaps if that had been lost, then there would have been nothing and he would have been lost completely.'

He thought about what I had suggested, and nodded. 'He's been through a lot – more than any of us could ever imagine.'

'Do you think she'd let you know if he – if he – '

'If he started to take it out on them? I doubt it: she never said anything to anyone before. We all knew what was happening, of course, but she herself never said anything. And you're sure the kid never said anything?'

'Mary? No, never.'

Again he seemed surprised, almost as though he had repeated the question in the hope of a different answer.

'Perhaps she thought things were going to be different,' I

suggested. 'Perhaps she didn't want to prejudice me against him before I got to know him.'

'Like me, you mean?'

I assured him that that was not what I meant. He apologised for the remark.

'I suppose if that's what Mary believed,' I said, 'then perhaps his wife might have thought things would have improved by the – '

'Yes; she did. That was why we . . .'

'I'm sorry, I didn't realise.'

'No, it was for the best. It was always him she wanted. And when she heard that he was alive after thinking him dead for so long I suppose she just began to hope for the best.'

'He might have changed,' I said in an attempt to console him.

He nodded.

'Is there anywhere, anywhere at all that they could all go to get away from here? Any other family, for instance?'

'There's only her mother, but she never really approved of the marriage, you see.'

He began to bait the hooks, speculating on his prospects and complaining at the calmness of the sea. I walked with him back to the water's edge, holding each reel as he spun the weighted line in increasing circles above our heads. We watched the slack line curve, and then splash, pulling taut as it entered the water and sank.

After a further silence, he turned to me and said, 'She never visited him, you know – all that time he was in London she never went to see him. She could have left the kids with any one of us, but she never did, not once.' He stopped abruptly, his words sounding too much like a plea. After that he crouched back down to the shingle, making himself comfortable and staring out to where his lines touched the water and disappeared.

The following morning, the man arrived at the lighthouse and waited in the doorway. I noticed him only when his shadow obscured the charts upon which I was working. I turned, looking instinctively for either his wife or daughter beside him.

'Not interrupting, am I?' He came into the room. 'Just give the order and I'll make my – myself scarce.' He grinned, stood to attention and saluted. 'I'm still in, you know. Still in His Majesty's Armed Forces.' He recited his name and service number, still standing to attention. I returned his salute, uncertain of his motives in forcing me into the exchange. He relaxed, watched me closely for a few seconds, and then burst into laughter, clapping his hands together and coming towards the table.

'Maps, is it?'

'Charts – of the fortifications. I was trying to calculate what still needs to be done in preparation for – '

'We had some map drawers with us at – ' He laughed again. 'Funny, that, I can't remember the bloody names. You'd think I'd never be able to forget them.' He hesitated and looked up from the plans to stare directly at me. 'On active service yourself, were you?' He exposed his teeth, his eyes still half closed.

'North Africa, Italy,' I said, still uncertain of his motives for asking.

'Not in the Far East, then?'

'No, I – '

'An officer?'

'Engineers.'

'A sapper!'

I nodded.

'But not one of the lads who got his hands dirty, eh?' I resented the remark, and was about to say so when he began to rub at his face and neck. 'Dry skin, see.' His tone changed and he studied his palm, holding out his hand to display the flakes of skin. 'They gave me some cream,' he said vaguely.

'I hope we didn't disturb you with the hammers,' I said, hoping to change the subject.

'Hammers?' He repeated the word several times, as though

building towards a joke. 'No, mate, never heard a thing. I was just having a look around the old place. Just refamiliarising myself.' He pronounced every syllable of the word, drawing it out. 'That's what they said I should do – refamiliarise myself.'

I nodded. Perhaps I was too conscious of his intrusion and what Donald Owen had told me, but he seemed almost to be goading me into an angry response, testing me with his changes of tone, his questions and contempt. Perhaps he sensed my unease and was taking advantage of it. And then he began to shake. I moved towards him, but he pushed out a hand to keep me away. After a few seconds, the trembling subsided.

'That's the bloody stuff they give me – all sorts of stuff.'

'I see.'

He moved around the table and leaned over the charts. 'They put an anti-aircraft battery in during the war, didn't they?'

'Yes, I was responsible for it. That's the remains of it out there.'

He turned to look through the doorway. His face clouded and he seemed unsure of something, disorientated. 'Yes, out there.' He pointed. Beside the houses, people moved. 'Out there.'

'Are you all right?' He appeared not to hear. I watched him carefully, trying to understand what he was seeing. He closed his eyes and stood perfectly still at the centre of the room.

'She's a good kid,' he said eventually, as though continuing a different conversation.

'Mary?'

He nodded, still staring towards the houses and moving figures. I was about to speak when he clapped his hands together and said, 'North Africa, eh? I was never in Europe, you know. Straight off to Singapore, I was. Did they tell you where I'd been?' His question accused me of knowing something I should not have done.

'I knew,' I said.

'And what else did they tell you?'

'Nothing. Just that you'd been taken prisoner, that you'd been in hospital in London, and that you were coming home. They've all been excited, looking forward to – '

'They?'

'Mary, your wife, the neighbours.'

'Been telling you, have they?' His insistence made me angry. Whatever I said he would turn against me.

A shout from one of the children distracted him. I offered him a cigarette, lighting two and passing one to him. He seemed grateful for the gesture, sat at the table, rubbed his face, and apologised. 'Sometimes I say things that I don't mean to say.' He watched my face to ensure I understood and believed him. 'Things never work out like you plan, and they've given me all sorts of stuff. Recurrent malaria, they said. That's what all this is.' He held out his arms and watched as they shook. 'Recurrent.'

I told him that I understood, and he began once again to rub his face as though the entire surface of his skin irritated him.

'I tell her that, but she doesn't know, see.'

I wanted to say something in the woman's defence, to explain how difficult things had been for her. But perhaps his own suffering had been too great for him to accept any comparisons. He continued to talk about her lack of understanding, continually asking if I thought he was right.

'It was her sent me up here,' he said after a pause.

'Oh?'

'Wanted to know if you'd got any tea, sugar, anything you could let her have until she gets straight and my back pay gets sorted out.'

I knew immediately that he was lying, that she would never have approached me with such a request regardless of how desperate she might have become.

'You know what women are,' he went on. 'One extra mouth to feed and always complaining.' He laughed and expected me to laugh with him. Instead I collected together what I could spare, knowing that what I was doing would embarrass her, and might destroy any of the trust she still had in me. I collected the tins and packets into a box, knowing that he would be unable to carry it. That way I would be able to return with him, telling lies of my own to hide his.

'Kids forever moaning about the things they can't have.'

'They always seemed content enough.'

'Naah, they're never satisfied. None of 'em know what it's like to go without.' He raised his arm again for me to study its thinness. I wondered how often he punished them with similar reminders of what he had become, of the things he had suffered.

'Appreciated the cigarettes you sent with the kid,' he said, indicating that I should add more to the provisions.

I tested the weight of the box, confident that he would be unable to lift it. As we moved towards the door, he blocked my way with his arm. Outside, I saw Mary, leaning against the wall where she had been waiting. She saw me and looked away. He shouted her to us.

'The kid'll take the box.'

She avoided my eyes as I gave it to her.

'Good kid, that. Do anything for her dad.' He touched her cheek and she flinched. I saw dark patches beneath her eyes. She walked away from us. He watched her, grinning at the success of his deception, the cigarette flicking up and down in his mouth.

'Appreciate it, mate.' And taking a step backwards, he saluted again, holding himself rigid, feet together, until I returned the gesture. Only the shaking cigarette betrayed him. He began to laugh, his eyes closed and then open and watching me. Turning, he followed his daughter across the uneven ground, his laughter dying in a drawn out bout of coughing as he approached her.

The children gathered at the water's edge, the boys prodding with sticks at something abandoned by the tide. The girls stood behind them, laughing and screaming as the canes were waved towards them. Mary stood apart, her brother by her side. Above the children hung a tight circle of gulls, rising and falling as they steadied themselves against the breeze.

Approaching, I saw the object of their attention to be a small shark, four or five feet long, sand-coloured and with a vague leopardskin pattern along its back. Its eyes had already been removed and its bloated belly seemed likely to burst at each prod. One of the boys lifted the slender tail and another propped the slack dorsal fin upright.

As I neared them they stood away from their find, watching me suspiciously, annoyed at my intrusion.

'It's been washed up,' one of the boys said. The others nodded.

I stopped beside Mary and her brother. 'It must have been left first thing,' she explained. 'We had one like it last year.' She pointed along the beach, her brother copying her actions and nodding vigorously. I wanted to ask her about her father, to let her know that I did not hold her responsible for the food he had taken. She left the small boy and walked to where the shark lay, its empty eyes already crawling with flies.

'We can have its teeth,' one of the boys announced, kneeling to lever open its mouth. The flies rose and resettled. Reasserting his claim over the body, the boy hit at it with a piece of driftwood. The belly slit open and a rope of white fell out. The girls screamed again. A red sac followed, in which the shape of an embryo shark was clearly visible. The boy chopped at the cord, and at each blow the girls turned away and covered their faces. The boys began to dance in a circle as the womb and unborn shark were detached and exhibited at arm's length on the piece of wood. From the shark's ruptured body spilled a liquid which filled the air with its smell, and which proved irresistible to the flies. The children became quiet, gathering to watch the stain seep into the shingle.

Above us the noise of the gulls grew louder. Individual birds dropped to the beach and stood around us. The boys threw pebbles, but the birds ignored them, screaming when hit, but only rising a few feet into the air before resettling.

'What will you do with it?' I asked.

'Last year we cut its head off and got its teeth. They were still in a bone.' She touched her jaw. Her brother did the same.

The boy with the unborn shark approached us. He offered it to Mary to inspect. Her brother began to cry and moved behind her.

'Aren't you going to have it?' the boy asked.

'The last one was the same,' she said to me, as though this explained everything. She whispered something to the boy. He looked up at me and then at the foot-long embryo curled on the wood. Without speaking he lowered the short plank to the beach and then sprang suddenly upright, grunting at the exertion. Automatically, I raised my arm to cover my face. Behind me the small boy screamed.

The unborn shark flew into the air, and when it hit the beach the gulls descended. The children applauded and ran shouting to reclaim their prize. Only Mary and her brother remained beside me, watching as I lowered my arm to see what had happened.

'We had engineers in some of the camps,' he said. Then he laughed – whether at a memory or a private joke I was uncertain. 'That's all you did then, is it – build things?'

I told him I was busy.

He smiled and sat opposite me at the table, laying his arms over the charts on which I was working. He had come uninvited into the room, using the blatant excuse that he wanted to ensure that I wasn't being disturbed by the children – using them, as he had used his daughter, for his own purposes.

He wore only his bottom set of teeth, constantly drawing back his lips and touching the top of his mouth with his tongue, flinching at its sensitivity. There were traces of blood in the exposed saliva, and he concluded each short sentence with a slapping sound which suggested that even to speak was causing him pain.

He waited for me to answer. When I did not, he said,

'You're friendly with Donald Owen. He was never called up, you know.'

'No, he told me.'

'Told you he was in the Merchant Marine, I suppose.'

'Yes.'

He laughed again. I was going to answer, when he began to cough, holding a hand over his mouth, pressing his thumb and forefinger into his cheeks as though in this way he might control the pain. And then he shouted at me, swore violently because of what I had witnessed. He moved to stand in the doorway, drawing a finger across his lips and studying the blood. 'None of you – ' he started to say, supporting himself against the wall. I moved towards him, pulling a chair and reaching out to steady him. When I touched him he pulled away and swore again. Even his anger, which might have provided him with some illusory release, caused him pain.

Shielding his eyes against the bright sunlight, he left.

I watched him cross the short distance to the houses. The men, too, stopped work to watch. I was afraid he might collapse, but knew that any further offer of help would only be refused as violently as before.

His wife appeared in the doorway as he negotiated the gate, kicking it open, still coughing, his hand still cupped over his mouth. She moved towards him, but he pushed her and she almost fell. She looked to the watching men and then followed him inside. I wondered what he would tell her, and what she would think of me as a result.

four

Tomorrow I will collect his body.

'I can come with you if you . . .'

I wait to see if she will finish, uncertain of why she has asked, her first words to me in almost three days. But she has stopped, and it is clear that she is giving voice to thoughts without thinking. I remain silent, unwilling to encourage her. Perhaps she thinks I have not heard, and is waiting for an answer. Perhaps she does not even realise she has spoken. She stands with crockery in her hands, and after a few seconds I hear it rattle as she lowers it into the sink, followed by the sound of splashing water.

It is evening, nine o'clock. The sun has set and the temperature of the room has fallen quickly.

I remain seated, watching her, unable to answer or console her. I see her shiver and leave the kitchen to close the windows. Suds fall from her hands and lie on the floor where they slowly dissolve.

I make a remark about the coolness, suggesting that the lawn might benefit from some attention. She nods and turns to look out, staring over the enclosed space, her hands held up like those of a surgeon awaiting gloves. She watches the thrushes hunting and chasing over the grass.

'What will it take you? Half an hour? An hour?'

'You can come if you're really sure.' I regret asking, surprised at her calm interruption of the silence.

She shakes her head. I nod, folding the newspaper across my lap. She sits opposite me, stroking the suds from her fingers and squeezing them to nothing. She has fine, slender hands and well cared-for nails. When we were first married she used to play the piano. It still stands in the other room, but its wires have lost their tension and she is too much of a perfectionist to want to play it now. I used to offer to have it repaired, and she in turn used to make a point of refusing.

Now her fingers move along the table like the legs of a spider testing the ground, slipping from side to side and smiling at a tune only she hears. She stops abruptly and turns them palm-upwards, twisting at her rings. She remarks that she has lost weight and holds out her left hand for me to see.

'We did the right thing,' I say. 'We had to insist on a private ceremony.'

She looks from her hands to mine. 'What time will you leave?'

'For the airfield? Midday.'

She nods, half turning to look back over the lawn, distracted by the movements of the cat as it drops from the wall, stopping mid-stride to watch us, perfectly still, only its curving tail betraying irritation at our presence. She watches, looking from the cat to the birds which stand around it, equally immobile and tensed.

With a large part of the foundations broken, I returned the pump to the Americans at Walsham. The anticipated seepage had never materialised. Even at a depth of six feet the soil remained sandy, full of pebbles, and easy to drain.

At the edge of the runway sat the same broken aircraft, its wing still providing the men beneath it with a cool place in which to sit and wait. We parked beside the disused tower and I went inside. I heard the voices of the two sergeants above me and shouted up to them. They had been drinking again, and complained good-naturedly at my interruption.

'We're going home!' one of them shouted as I entered the room. 'End of November. Home, home, home. One hundred per cent certain.' He pointed his bottle at a sheet of paper pinned to the wall.

'Both of you?'

'Every last one of us!'

'Congratulations.'

They looked at each other and laughed. I pointed through the window to the waiting lorry and pump.

'Keep it! Tip it in the ocean!'

'Sea,' I corrected, causing more laughter.

'Yeah, tip it in the sea.'

'And what about the base? Is it going to be used when you've gone?'

'Who cares?' They laughed again and lifted more bottles from a bucket beneath the table.

'What about the aircraft?'

'They've been sold.'

'Sold?'

'Don't ask us – that's all they told us. Who cares?' This time I laughed with them.

'You got long to go on the wrecking – the, er, demolition?'

'Another two, three weeks.'

'And then what? You staying on?'

'In the Army, you mean? Yes.'

'Doing what?'

I told them that I didn't know, that I would probably be posted to undertake a similar task elsewhere. But they were too excited at their own good news to remain interested in what might happen to me.

One of them stood and raised his bottle above his head. 'Four years of not knowing, and we're finally going Stateside. Finally going. No-vem-ber.'

Even the man whose wife had been killed was unable to suppress his excitement, smiling and slapping the table with both palms.

'And I suppose you intend drinking away all your rations before you leave.'

'Why not!'

I mimicked their accents and they shook their bottles, showering me with foam.

Afterwards, we stood at the small-paned window and looked down at the expanse of concrete, at the broken silver aircraft scattered like toys, and at the massive domed sheds with their impenetrable shadows. The men beneath the wing ran in circles, throwing a ball against the fuselage and erupting into cheers.

'Too warm for running around,' the man beside me said. I agreed with him.

'Will the two of you keep in touch do you think?'

'With each other?'

They turned to face each other, both uncertain.

'Yeah, sure.'

'Yeah, we'll have reunions. Get our' – he was going to say 'wives' – 'get ourselves into a bar someplace and – ' He patted the other man on the shoulder. I knew then that after leaving the base neither of them would make the effort, that they would never meet.

'Hear you got your own celebrity,' the man who had lost his wife said. He said it to cover his friend's awkwardness.

'Celebrity?'

'Guy come back from the Jap prison camp.'

'Oh, yes.'

'We had a kid work for a time in the ambulance depot. Said he was there when the truck from London arrived.'

'Well, I'd hardly call him a celebrity.'

'What! Guy comes back from three–four years in a camp. Stateside he'd be a celebrity.'

'Yeah. How is he, okay?'

'I daresay he could be, given time.'

'Bad, uh?'

I nodded. 'Nobody seems very certain.'

'He talk about it?'

'Not to me. I don't – '

'Yeah, takes 'em like that, I suppose.'

The other nodded. 'Singapore, the kid reckoned.'

After that we sat in silence, listening to the shouting men and the hollow sound of the ball against the plane.

'They used to mean a lot, some of those machines.' He spoke affectionately, the memory rising above his half drunken excitement. 'We'd stay up all night to keep 'em moving, keep 'em flying.'

The other nodded, crossing to join him by the window, looking down at the discarded aircraft, like silver crosses along the line of the runway. The drink had made them maudlin and nostalgic, draining their memories before beginning anew.

'Do your families know you're going home?'

Both nodded. Now there was no excitement, only a sadness as they thought about their homes and their years away from them.

'I'm going to Denver. Live with my brother,' the one who had lost his wife said.

'Denver ain't far,' added the other.

'No, not far. Seven, maybe seven hundred and fifty miles. No distance at all.'

I agreed with them both, embarrassed by my intrusion, by the lies my presence forced them into telling.

'But seriously, what about the pump?'

'Have it!'

'Yeah, take it.' They spoke loudly, relieved at the change of subject.

'But won't anybody want to know where it's gone?'

They smiled. 'So they want to know. You think they're going to come looking for one lousy pump with all this and God knows what else falling to pieces?' He waved his arm towards the window.

'No, I suppose not.' My thanks – although I had no further use for the machine – initiated another round of drinks, and they insisted on giving me an unopened box containing two dozen bars of chocolate 'for the kids'.

'It's one of the kids' father who's come back?'

'Yes, the father of the girl.'

'November twenty-eight,' one of them shouted, and

suddenly they were excited again, waving their arms and shouting, spilling their drinks and banging their fists onto the table.

Before I left, they made me a further present of a fishing rod and reel. I insisted I could not accept, but they would not listen, surprised at my genuine attempts to refuse it. They had, they explained, bought the rods in Lincoln and had been able to sell the remainder of their equipment back to the same dealer. 'Wouldn't take that one back, though.' They shared an obvious wink, and I took the rod.

'But what about when you get home? There are seas – oceans – all around America.'

'You ever been to Denver?' They exploded in a burst of uncontrollable laughter.

As I left they walked with me to the lorry, banging its doors as we drove away. The men beneath the wing emerged to watch us, cheering and waving and chasing each other in and out of the shadow. It was almost three months to their departure, but now the time left to wait seemed suddenly not to matter.

At weekly intervals following his return, the ambulance arrived to take Mary's father to hospital in Lincoln. The two attendants stood and talked as he prepared himself, allowing him to sit between them in the cab. Often, he made a great play of keeping them waiting until a small crowd had gathered to see him off. They wished him well and waved, and he shouted back and ordered the men to leave.

The arrival of the van often coincided with the arrival of the morning transport, and the men, uncertain at first of how to react to him, were quickly reassured by his appearance and the casual manner in which he spoke to them. I knew it was an act, but it was the way they all behaved in the company of other men. They shared with him the bond of common soldiers, and beyond their sympathy for him they respected him for what he had been through. This he took advantage of. They offered him cigarettes and shared their jokes and complaints with him. He in turn expressed feelings none of them would have dared to admit to in my presence. His wife and children stood apart, watching as he prolonged the ceremony of climbing into the van and leaving.

I overheard one of the men admit that his appearance seemed to belie his strength, and that he was surprised at the man's constant use of foul language in the presence of the women and children – something the others were all careful to avoid. Such language was not uncommon amongst them, but they were seldom careless with it. Perhaps they believed, as I did, that such superficial affectation would have been stripped from him. I had seldom heard him swear, but that, I suspected, was the result of the fact that he regarded me as someone separate from them, as an officer to be excluded from their common camaraderie. Or perhaps, after his long imprisonment, swearing was his way of appearing normal to them.

Other than his appearance at the arrival of the van, they saw little of him. During the day, he remained indoors, emerging only in the evenings to walk over the site with Mary or to sit beside the doorway and join the communal conversations. This, I noticed, often had the effect of destroying those gatherings, the others moving back indoors with their excuse of unfinished tasks or the growing coolness of the evenings.

Just as Mary rarely spoke in his presence, so his wife remained silent, and when she did speak he took every opportunity to contradict her or to make a joke of what she said. This and his language alienated the other women and their husbands, none of whom spoke out in her defence. Their genuine concern prior to his return had evaporated along with their own expectations of his condition and behaviour.

The frequency of his nervous convulsions seemed to decrease, and only once did I see his wife kneel to hold his arms, shouting for Mary before managing to lead him indoors. Some of the women had watched, unable to either help or understand.

The two ambulance attendants made a great fuss of him, and

he introduced them by their first names to his wife. I remembered what the Americans had said about his status as a celebrity, and wondered if he, too, had expected as much. The attendants told her of his improvement as though paying her a personal compliment.

On one occasion, a month after his return, the men left the van a hundred yards from the road's end, the driver walking to the houses whilst his partner remained in the cab. Both saw me and waved.

'Not working today?' the driver asked as we met. I told him that we were, but that the lorries had not yet arrived. This seemed to please him, and turning he beckoned to his partner to bring the van forward. 'Only we didn't want to come too close on account of the drills,' he explained. 'We've got another bloke on. He's in the back. Stretcher.' He whispered the last word and shook his head. I told him I understood, and that I would delay the start of the machines until they had departed. The van arrived behind us and they exchanged a series of gestures and knowing looks. The driver crossed to the houses, and I waited, instinctively lowering my voice as I spoke to the man in the cab.

He smiled, nodded over his shoulder and said, 'He can't hear you. Hasn't heard nor said a thing these past two years.'

'Oh, I'm sorry.'

'Sorry? No, no need. He's happy enough. Not many – '

The driver reappeared, signalling to us. Ahead of him walked Mary's father, insisting loudly that his daughter be allowed to accompany him, that she would make the journey sitting on his knee. Seeing me beside the van, he looked for signs of the others, demanding to know where they were, why they weren't there to see him off. The driver asked Mary if she wanted to go with them.

'Of course she does, I've told you!' He took her arm and pulled her towards the road. The driver agreed and climbed into the cab. Mary started to follow him, but her father pulled her back down, insisting that they wait until the arrival of the men, 'his mates'. The driver looked to me for support, and I explained that the lorries were likely to be some considerable time.

From the rear of the van came the sound of something being dropped. Leaving the cab, the driver opened the rear doors, motioning with his arms before closing them gently and walking back to where we waited.

Mary's father moved away from the van, demanding that his daughter did the same. His wife appeared in the doorway, watching us, uncertain of what was happening.

The situation was eased by the arrival of the lorries. Pushing his daughter ahead of him, he came back to the road, laughing and pointing as though he had won an argument or wager. He accused me of having lied about the delay. 'Good blokes, these,' he shouted, applauding the arrival of the first of the men. Watching him, it was as though the events of the previous few minutes had never taken place.

The men climbed down, and once again he became the centre of attention, pointing to his daughter, explaining to them what had happened. But they seemed less concerned than usual, tired, perhaps, of his demands, of the feelings he exploited. They gave him cigarettes – which he made his usual great act of accepting – and then they left him, dispersing onto the site to collect their tools and begin work.

He shouted after them, angry that they had ignored him. Dividing the cigarettes, he gave some to his wife to keep for his return. Mary climbed into the cab and waited. She alone, it seemed, could draw him away. He pulled himself into the seat, positioning himself beneath her, pulling her into his lap and holding his arm around her waist.

The van left, and I turned to the woman. She continued to wave, the cigarettes still bunched in her hand. The younger children emerged from the houses to stand beside her. I shouted to her, but she seemed not to hear.

The delay, and the men's behaviour towards the man, had been caused by the posting of new orders, which meant that the majority of them would be employed doing similar work to that at Cable Point for their remaining months of service.

This in turn fuelled their sense of resentment and grievance – against their work, against me, and against Cable Point and all it represented.

It did not occur to me until later that the patient in the rear of the van could not have been deaf, as the attendants believed, if the sound of the drills and hammers was likely to upset him.

five

Alone, Michael and I discussed his intention of leaving the Army in a year's time. She knew nothing of this, and neither of us told her. He confessed to being frightened, uncertain of what he wanted and of what the Army was doing to him. I told him I understood, and he believed me.

For the first time, we discussed and compared our experiences, and I realised how little I really knew of the life he was living. Even in the Army I had had a trade, something with which I was equipped to earn a living beyond the secure confines of military life, and which, eventually, was to prove more attractive than that life. With him it was different: he was leaving not because of the lure of something better, but because of the simple and frightening realisation that he had lost control of what was happening to him. He was twenty-seven, the same age I had been in 1946. The realisation surprised me and I mentioned it to him.

He did not intend to remain at home, nor did he plan to marry the girl in London, who by now had become pregnant by him, and with whom he had been spending much of his leave. This, I suspect, only compounded his confusion, forcing him into decisions he was reluctant to make. His greatest fear, it seemed, was his uncertainty that when the time came to decide whether or not to leave the Army, he would be drawn back, away from the girl and into the ordered and secure life it was preparing for him. This I understood only too well.

His time in Ireland only served to heighten that fear, to provide it with a tangible focus, giving each day the simplest of objectives, each minor success becoming the cause for more and more celebration. He began to drink. There might also have been drugs. I can't be certain. I wanted him to confide in me because I wanted to let him know that I understood. Perhaps he really had become careless. Perhaps the captain had known this and had wanted to be able to tell me. Perhaps his carelessness had placed the lives of others in jeopardy.

On one occasion he confessed to having been violently sick at something he had seen. He confessed also to a recurrent nightmare in which he killed a line of children, their heads hooded, singing nursery rhymes as they threw bottles of petrol, childishly applauding their results, burning men racing past him. He laughed nervously as he told me, avoiding my eyes, as though his forced manner might suppress or deny his true feelings. He asked me about my own experiences and the things I had seen. I spoke of some of them for the first time, surprised at the vividness of each memory, at the ease with which they returned after thirty years.

When we parted he shook my hand and held it, about to say something, but releasing his grip and turning away as she came into the room behind us.

As we waited beside the train I remember thinking how remarkably similar in appearance he was to myself at the same age. She had long since laid claim to his good looks, but there was something in the way he held himself and the way he walked which I recognised. Perhaps it was the Army moulding us, strengthening our backs and shoulders as it destroyed other parts we knew nothing about.

His letters continued to arrive, and I continued to search them for indications of his true feelings, of how he was coping with his fear. Sometimes it seemed to have been dispelled completely . . . and then he would say something – something he had done or seen, something about the acts committed by other soldiers – and I would know.

Under my father's command in the Great War there had been boys of sixteen and seventeen, there illegally, of course, but encouraged and congratulated all the same. He had known about them, but had done nothing to have them removed and sent home. They were just children, younger perhaps than some of those confronting my own son. I wonder if he felt any qualms in driving them ahead of him at Arras and Vimy, or at any of the other silver-written names engraved beneath his – my – regimental coat of arms. There were children on the television news reports – thin, poorly dressed and outlined in black against fires, waiting to inflict whatever injury they believed might lead towards the useless victory none of them understood.

In the letters were reports of football matches, of dances, of his friends, of visiting celebrities and politicians. I wished for his sake that he did not have to write such letters.

He showed me a piece of paper upon which his name had been written and underlined in pencil. I asked him what it meant. He explained that every morning they would find several such strips of paper Sellotaped to the corrugated iron gates of their command post, placed there during the night by someone brave enough to expose themself to the scaffolding platform and blinding white lights which swept the street. Sometimes the names were accompanied by death threats or the home addresses of soldiers and the names of their parents, brothers or sisters. He told me that it was considered lucky to leave the armoured patrol cars, walk the street and tear down the strip containing your own name: that way, he said, it was easier to believe that the threat had been removed. Sometimes pieces of paper would remain attached to the gates for days and the men whose names they contained would isolate themselves, shunned and frightened. He told me there had been several strips containing his own name. Once, a close friend had been shot in the leg as he inspected this sinister 'notice board'. Ironically, his own name had not been present.

For his sake, I resisted the temptation to ask if any other details had been 'posted'.

During that same leave he told me of the men who were returned to England as unfit for service – still cowards in a war where concepts of cowardice and heroism had become ridiculously inapplicable.

He told me also of the men who had deserted, either across the border or whilst on leave. They were seldom successful, he said, but their actions served their purpose. Often they were imprisoned for little more than the length of their remaining service, unwanted and despised where so much depended on the actions of so many others. I asked him outright if he had ever considered such a course. He laughed at the suggestion and shook his head. I told him I believed him, but I knew he was lying. Perhaps this was why he had become careless.

He asked me if I had ever believed my own life to be in danger during the war. I answered him honestly that I had not, that the greatest danger had come from weakened buildings collapsing as we cleared them. I told him about a booby-trapped archway in Berlin where a large explosive charge had failed to denotate, even beneath the bulldozer upon which I rode. He laughed, and I remembered my own father's death, reflecting afterwards on how perversely history had repeated itself.

Towards the middle of September I received the revised plans for the new station. Although not responsible for the construction of the buildings, it was now important to ensure that the correct foundations had been prepared. Consequently, I reorganised my schedule. With the plans came those for the line of new housing, half a mile north of the present terrace, and linked to the site by a new road.

Several days later three men arrived to study the site. These were the architects and engineers responsible for the reconstruction. They stood together, unrolling plans and pointing to the corresponding outline over the ground. One of them paced out distances around the site and the children followed him, mimicking his strides and shouting out their own measurements. The others laughed, but the man turned and swore, retracing his steps. The inhabitants came onto the road to watch, their shared glances expressing the same anxiety as when the two Americans had arrived. The men asked me about them, unconcerned when I told them of their worries and their need for reassurance. Mary stood with her mother, neither of them joining the speculations of the other women about why the men were there.

I became angry at the way the men spoke of the inhabitants as a nuisance to be removed, and at the assumption that I shared their views.

The children left the site and waited by the Light. Mary joined them, leaving her mother standing alone. Behind her, the sun barely penetrated the dark interior of her home. There was no sign of her husband. Several days previously I had seen a bruise on the woman's face and listened to her excuses of how she had received it. Now she ignored me, turning away at my greeting.

The men continued to pace out their distances, shouting to each other and writing their calculations in notebooks. Following a brief conference, the man in charge informed me that over nine hundred square yards of ground would have to be re-excavated and filled more solidly. This, too, made me angry.

The children ran around us, whooping like Red Indians before dispersing into the chaos of brick and concrete. He told me that I should keep them away, that the site was unsafe. Then he shouted at them and walked alone back to the waiting car. The women watched him, their faces hard and emotionless like those of their fishwife ancestors.

When the men had gone I walked towards the houses, preparing to explain the reason for their visit. The women watched as I approached, but as I emerged at the road they turned away and entered their homes. The gap between us was widening and I, too, had become an impostor. More importantly, they now saw the challenge to my own authority, my inability to control what was about to happen to them. In their eyes I had played at being powerful and I had betrayed them.

Only Mary's mother still stood beside her door, trapped between me and what remained inside. I heard coughing, and she shouted to her daughter, beckoning vigorously for her to hurry. I decided against offering to help and turned away.

'They went straight past us, thousands of 'em, all on bicycles. Fifty miles a day they must have made.' He slid his upright palm across the table, raising it and slamming it down. Contrary to my expectations, it did not disturb him to discuss what had happened.

'Was it in Singapore itself that you were captured?'

'Surrendered, you mean. No, we were twenty miles north. Mainland. Reconnaissance.' Everyone else had carefully avoided the subject, but with me he seemed almost relieved to be able to talk. It was not until much later that I understood his reasons for doing so.

On several occasions he remembered something too painful to repeat, and so instead he became angry, perversely accusing me with his gestures and tone of not wanting to know, of interfering. I thought he might become violent, but his brief rages subsided into fits of shaking or coughing which bent him double and left him gasping for breath. He swore, spitting heavy balls of phlegm into the sand.

'Nobody wants to know – not really.' He spoke as though he had only just arrived at the realisation. 'Forgotten bloody Army they called us. Well, they're still managing to forget. What chance have I got? Tell me, what bloody chance have I got?' Beneath his anger there was genuine concern, but he would not confess it for fear of being thought weak.

'Have you discussed it with your wife?'

'Her! It's me I'm talking about. Me! It's me who's got to make a living and set things straight. Before, there was at least' – he waved his hand over the site – 'but now . . .'

'You could move to Lincoln, to the re-training – '

'Been talking to her, have you?' he said sarcastically.

I shook my head, refusing to rise to his challenge.

He clenched his fists, and once again I became aware of the power of which his deceptively frail body might still be capable. He began to have difficulty breathing, banging his chest and producing more phlegm. His frustration, I guessed, was made worse by the realisation that he had been betrayed by his own body, that it would no longer support his anger, weakening him from within, stripping down his ability to resist, his ability to do anything positive towards reasserting himself. Until he was in a position to do that, the only ones likely to suffer were his family – the only ones over whom he still maintained any control. Realising this – the fact that he probably had more control over them than he did of himself, allied to his unpredictability – worried me. It was almost as though the will to fight exerted itself for its own sake – for the sake of proving to himself and others that the man he had once been was still alive. In the confines of his home that violence – however frustrated by his physical condition – was spent destructively and against the only ones who were in a position to help him recover. He might have returned to a supportive community and home, but by his own indifference and hostility he had only alienated and isolated himself further. And as he did so he clung increasingly to his daughter, playing on his weakness and her expectations, demanding that she accompany him, exhibiting their forced friendship as an indication of his ability to recover.

Belligerence had been his comfort, and this he had confused with the will to recover, replaced now by simple bitterness as his resentment and frustration increased, and as his targets became fewer.

In the short time he had been back he had dominated Mary's life almost entirely, refusing to see what, at fifteen, she was struggling to achieve for herself. To him she was still the eleven-year-old child he had left behind. In his presence she behaved childishly. He treated her as a child, and in doing so he mistook her acquiescence for willingness.

Sitting opposite me, he began to laugh, shaking his head, his eyes closed. I waited for him to explain, but he did not, simply turning to face me and saying I wouldn't understand. On his lip I saw the line of red where the false teeth still caused his gums to bleed. He plucked at the skin of his arm, drawing it taut before releasing it and watching it fall back into place. It was no longer supple, and red marks showed where he had held it.

He had expected more, and then destroyed what little hope or encouragement people had been prepared to offer. We were constantly reassured of the efforts being made to help him and of his eventual recovery, and though I did not doubt that the doctors were doing everything they could for him, I knew that their treatment would not work and that he was attempting to reassert himself, to reclaim some part of his old self independently of their efforts. This also worried me. If what Donald Owen had told me was true, then the only recognisable characteristic which his ordeal had not destroyed – his unpredictable violence – was very likely the one which would reassert itself first. Perhaps he too realised this and sought to display rather than disguise the fact as further evidence of his recovery.

He watched me through the smoke of his cigarette, smiling at my uncertainty and discomfort. Then he looked up to the pale sky, closing his eyes and letting the smoke rise in a plume into the still air.

It was now mid-September, and as the nights began to draw in, so too did the mist which hung over the sea. It arrived swiftly and dramatically, rolling in a solid sheet to cover the houses and demolition site in only a few minutes. From the glass collar of the Light I was able to look down upon it and watch as it levelled the uneven ground like the leading wave of a new tide. Even from my vantage point I could not see the lights of the houses, only the movement at the mist's upper surface where their warm smoke rose to disturb and reinforce it.

Sound, too, became subdued: only occasionally did I hear the children or the gulls or the whooping siren calls of passing ships warning of their position and course.

It was on one such evening that Donald Owen invited me into his home.

The house was the same size as the others, but seemed larger as a result of being more sparsely furnished and containing no additional ornamentation. It smelled of fish, drying wood and tobacco, and was dimly lit. Two cats lay in the untidy hearth, their heads resting only inches from the low fire.

He shook some coal from a wicker basket. 'Sea coal,' he said. 'At least we call it sea coal to disguise the fact that it's washed up from sunken coal carriers.'

In one corner of the room stood a mound of driftwood and whole crates still with their illegible stencilled markings. The room was warm, and I welcomed his invitation after the cold of the lighthouse.

'They'll be wanting to put some kind of heating system in when they come to refurbish the Light,' he said, smiling at my complaints and inviting me closer to the fire. 'When it was an oil lamp they used to sit around the bowl. You could see their shapes against it.'

We spent most of the evening discussing our futures, and he told me about life at Cable Point between the wars, of its simplicity, and then of the changes and unrest as the old families died or left and were replaced.

' "Between the wars",' he said reflectively, repeating the phrase until its full meaning became clear, suggesting that in the future all time would be marked like this.

We ate a meal of tinned meat and bread. He produced a bottle of whisky and showed me a crate containing eight more. He was an assured, generous man, the only one who seemed capable of existing independently of what was happening at Cable Point; the one most likely to be the least affected by the drastic changes about to take place. He told me of his plans to return to South Wales, to work in the Cardiff docks or to re-enlist in the Merchant Marine. He seemed unconcerned about his enforced departure, confident in his ability to live elsewhere and find another job.

The mist rose against the window, obscuring completely anything we might have seen, throwing back our reflections when we tried. This, too, did not bother him, and he laughed at my frequent exclamations at its density.

Against one wall stood a wireless set which glowed with the names of a hundred cities, and which filled the small room with static and a dozen unintelligible languages as he turned the dial. It was a powerful receiver, one he had brought with him from a ship upon which he had worked.

'Some nights,' he said hesitantly, 'I just sit and listen to the foreign stations. Can't understand a bloody word they're saying, mind, but I enjoy the noise.' He laughed and said that I must think him stupid.

In the silence between stations I heard voices from the neighbouring house, Mary's home. He listened and turned the dial more rapidly, embarrassed, in my presence, at being able to overhear.

'It's him,' he said as the voices rose above the music. 'Paper-thin, these walls; you can hear every word some nights.'

I knew that the stone walls were solidly built, and that he was making excuses for the man. He adjusted the volume, but the signal was weak, and did little to disguise the sound of the raised voice.

'Every night?' I asked without looking up at him.

He understood and nodded. His feelings of affection for the woman had been replaced by those of sympathy, pity almost.

'Mind you, it's nothing new: he used to shout at her before he went off.' Thus we made our excuses for the man; excuses also for our own reluctance to intervene, our own helplessness. Individual words became clearly audible, and I, too, felt embarrassed at overhearing, at being with him.

'Do you think the doctors in Lincoln know he's like this?'

'I doubt it.'

He nodded.

'Do any of the others overhear?'

'I shouldn't think so,' he said. 'The house on the other side's empty, remember.'

'I suppose the children know,' I said.

'I don't see how they could miss it.'

'Would you have married her if he had been killed, do you think?' I regretted asking the question, but he seemed pleased at the opportunity to speculate. Only I had ever asked him, ever suggested the prospect.

'No, I doubt it. It was the circumstances as much as anything . . .'

'So despite everything, you think she'll stay with him?'

He nodded. 'She wouldn't know how to leave him. She'd be lost without him. She's known nothing else, you see.' It was as simple and as tragic as that.

The voice continued through the wall, and during the silences we waited expectantly. Occasionally the shouting was broken by drawn out bouts of painful coughing and then longer silences. I imagined the woman and girl in the same room, waiting for him to continue, constrained to participate.

'Since they came here she's never really been anywhere else.'

I watched his face, saw him tense as the shouting increased.

'He shouldn't call her those things, not names like that.'

I wondered if he had ever banged on the wall to let her know that he was aware of what was happening. 'Does she know you can hear?'

He shrugged.

'You haven't told her?'

'No. I think that telling her would only make things worse for her: it's bad enough that she has to suffer these things without her knowing that someone else is aware of what's happening.'

'I suppose so. You don't think he might do something?'

'To her you mean?'

'To either of them.'

'I don't know.' He had clearly considered the possibility.

'But you think he's capable of it?'

He shook his head and then began to nod.

'And all the doctors see is what he shows them. Is that it?'

He nodded again. 'I sometimes think that it would take something like that to happen before anybody will take notice of what's happening. He shouldn't be here! Can't they see that by being here he's literally living in a world of his own making? As far as he's concerned nothing's changed. Unless something happens to make them realise what's happening, he'll just continue to take advantage of her, of everybody, and things will be exactly the same as before.'

'How do the other neighbours feel?'

He laughed coldly. 'Oh, they wanted to help, wanted to be sympathetic towards him – for her sake if not for his – but seeing him like – '

Outside, a door slammed and we waited, listening.

'It's the girl I feel sorry for,' he went on. 'She'll end up just like her mother if this goes on for much longer. She's caught in the middle, you see.'

'Yes. It's a pity the two of them – she and her mother – can't work together towards trying to improve things. I'm sure if they let him see that they were capable of existing without him, then he'd have to start behaving differently towards them.'

He smiled at the naivety of my solution. 'I think perhaps they would have done if him and Mary hadn't been so close. It's funny that, but she was always ready to come round to him no matter how badly he treated her. And in his absence, I suppose, she was forced into taking on too many responsibilities.'

'You think she resents her mother because of that?'

'I think she's gone back to him without really knowing what's happened. She used to tell such tales, to expect so much of him, that I think sometimes she sees him as she expected him to be and not as he is.'

'It would explain a great deal,' I said.

'But it still doesn't help matters; makes them worse, in fact.'

I agreed with him. Many of my own suspicions had been confirmed, and I was able to understand the relationship between mother, father and daughter more clearly.

'If only she was a bit stronger,' he said, meaning the woman.

'I suppose she, too, had her expectations, her hopes that things were going to be different, better.'

'Oh, she had those all right. But that's the problem, you see: she's spent four years just waiting and looking forward to his return. She's let herself forget how bad things really were; and like the kid, she'd built up her own picture of how good things were going to be when he came back.'

We spent the remainder of the evening discussing our lives before arriving at Cable Point. The shouting had stopped, but in the silence we strained for the slightest sound.

As I left he returned to the wireless, standing with his hands to the dying fire and his face close to the cloth speaker and its undecipherable confusion of reassuring noises.

six

I left the Chapel of Rest and at the door he shook my hand,
smiling to reassure me, his grip professionally firm, letting me
know that he was in complete control. In the panels of
coloured glass set into the door was the bearded face of Jesus
with his questioning hands held by his cheeks. Elsewhere
there were red and yellow tulips and a Latin inscription that I
did not understand.

She was waiting in the car, and I saw her turn to watch as
we came out. He looked to where she sat and we exchanged a
nod of understanding. The arrangements are complete: he will
come to the house, and from there the coffin will be taken to
the cemetery.

The costs of the funeral have been hidden from me at every
step. I ask, but he simply smiles and tells me not to worry. It
is not because he is ashamed of revealing his prices, simply
that death and its cost do not go well together in the same
conversation. I spare his professional pride by agreeing with
him as often as possible. This is what he is accustomed to: grief,
not death, is his profession.

In the Chapel of Rest there had been another coffin,
smothered with flowers and ringed by mourners, old people,
mourning their own remaining lives as much as that invisibly
extinguished within the box around which they sat. One of
the women looked up and smiled as I passed the door and

glanced in. Perhaps she thought I was there to make arrangements for my father. The others watched her and looked
severe. I guessed that the body was that of her husband. Her
grief seemed less sincere surrounded by the temporary, public
displays of the others.

In his office he had asked me about the room in which the
coffin would spend the night. He advised me to draw the
curtains and to ensure that it be kept as cool as possible. I told
him that this had already been done, that she had prepared the
room the day before. He clapped his hands together once, as
though about to applaud.

He asked me about the arrangements I had made for the
collection of the coffin. I outlined the details as I understood
them – that two men and transport had been detailed to
return with me from the airfield. He seemed relieved when I
explained that we had refused the Army's offer of a military
burial. He enquired about the route taken by the bearers out
of the house. I explained about the french windows and the
wide path to the road. He nodded and rose, indicating that
our interview was at an end.

Now we stand in the doorway, beside Jesus, his closed eyes
and questioning hands. It is a knowing, comforting gesture.
We shake hands and I look to where she waits, her head
bowed, not wanting to look up and see us. The coloured glass
reflects the sun, shining in circles and black lines across his
white shirt and sober tie. The face of Jesus is imprinted on his
cheek. He does not seem to notice, and I do not mention it.

Behind the engraved, opaque glass of the adjoining window I
can make out the indistinct forms of the old people, mourning
as only they know how, comfortable in their collective display
of sorrow and remorse.

I walk towards the car, waiting on the road for a line of
traffic to pass. She is silent, studying her eyes and lips in the
mirror.

The first of the autumn storms coincided with our start on the
final phase of demolition. The sky remained overcast for much

159

of the day and clouds the colour of pewter hung in a low curtain over the horizon. Seen through them, the sun became an indistinct orange ball.

The men of Cable Point spent much of the day on the beach, dragging their small boats up the shingle and into the dunes.

In the afternoon, Donald Owen arrived at the lighthouse and suggested that I secured all the doors and windows, and that the machinery on the site was moved into more sheltered positions. With him I inspected the tapering walls of the tower, plucking at the plates of crumbling stucco loosened by the heat.

On the site, the men constantly stopped working, holding out their palms in expectation of rain, feeling it before it came. And when it did eventually arrive they cheered, climbing out of the deeper excavations and running for shelter.

Without the sun, the site looked even more like that of an abandoned city awaiting rediscovery, its lines and squares washed clean of their camouflage of sand, its obscured colours becoming once again distinct. Rusted supports rose through the debris, giving the impression that something was being built rather than destroyed. I was reminded of my satisfaction at seeing the fortifications constructed, at raising the low buildings and steep defensive slopes from blueprints and sheets of scribbled calculations. Then, upon completion, there had been a brief ceremony, and we had departed before the arrival of the gun crews. Now, looking over what remained, it was difficult to believe that any of those guns had ever fired a shot in anger, or even that a war had taken place.

I watched the men as they resumed work, seemingly invigorated by the downfall. They pointed to the sun's returning brilliance and to the crystalline blue sky which followed the grey. Despite their earlier resentment and frustration, they now seemed proud of their achievement. It was almost as if by breaking down the solid structures in readiness for something new, something designed to protect rather than to take life, they were exorcising from their minds and bodies the final traces of something which had haunted us all. Perhaps if I had been able to exhaust myself physically on the same task, then I too might have shaken off those traces and the memory of what was to happen there.

I saw the children emerge from where they had been sheltering. A boy carried the body of one of the site's stray cats. There was no mark on the corpse, but I knew from the way they responded to my greeting that they blamed the demolition work for the cat's death. One of the younger children informed me of their intention to bury it. I asked where. He began to tell me, but the boy with the body stopped him.

'Up in the foundations of the old lighthouse?' I guessed, pointing in the direction of the dunes.

He nodded and looked down to the animal cradled in his arms.

'We bury all sorts of things up there,' the small boy said.

'Beneath the sand in the well?'

He nodded. 'Gulls and sometimes sea swallows.'

'I see.'

'We find them,' he added quickly, guiltily. 'We find them already killed.' The others nodded vigorously. Only the boy holding the cat remained still, watching me.

'It's been killed with a hammer,' he said accusingly.

I felt the body. There was no sign of broken skin or bone. 'I doubt it; it's probably been abandoned or starved.'

'A hammer!' he repeated, and they began to move away, satisfied. I decided not to press my point.

A door slammed and Mary came towards us, causing the others to regroup and await her arrival. The boy handed her the cat and she sat with it, stroking it and plucking at its wet fur.

'Her father's gone to Lincoln,' the boy said, as though explaining something I did not understand.

'Yes, I know.'

'You know everything!' Mary shouted, dropping the cat and standing to face me. I apologised. She left us and walked further into the rubble. The others remained together, the younger boys beginning to argue over who should carry the cat. One of them began to beat at the body with a slender cane. I followed her, stopping behind her.

161

'He says he won't have to go back to the hospital for much longer.'

'Is that what he told you?'

She nodded. 'He said you think we're a charity case.'

'A what?'

'A charity case. He said that you were an officer, and that officers were always sticking their noses into things.' She hesitated, turning to watch my reaction. I tried to understand whether she wanted me to deny what he had told her, or if she was repeating what he had said with the simple intention of hurting me and proving to me the growing strength of the bond between them.

'I might be an officer, but I'm not *his* officer. He isn't in the Army now, you know.'

'He is! He said that if he wanted to he could stay in. Then he said that we could all go and live with him at a new Army camp somewhere else. He said we didn't need nobody's charity.'

I shrugged. I knew that even she was only half convinced by what he had told her, and I remained unwilling to present myself as a target for her own violent and uncertain emotions. Whatever might have existed between us during the early weeks of my stay had by now been severely strained by her accusations and his unpredictable demands upon us both.

She climbed down from the low wall upon which she had been sitting and came towards me, her arms folded beneath her breasts, accentuating their outline. Then she held her arms behind her back and looked much younger.

'What did he mean by "charity case"?' I asked again.

'It was after you'd given us that box of food. He told her that you were doing it on purpose to make it look as though he couldn't look after us. He said you were all the same. He told her that he'd told you we didn't want the food and that we could manage all right without it. He made her cry and asked us all about what else you'd been giving her.'

I fought to control my anger. Had she understood the hidden meaning, the implications of what he had said? She, I knew, had overheard our entire transaction.

'And did you eat the food?'

She turned away to avoid answering.

'And does he smoke the cigarettes I give him? Bloody right
he does!' I stopped myself. It was the first time I had sworn in
her presence and I hated him for what he was forcing me to do,
to become. There was no one now, except him, to whom she
might turn. Even if she had not believed what he had said about
me she would never admit to it now, and in her anger and
disillusionment whatever he told her would become the truth.

She turned to face me, opening and closing her mouth,
concentrating on the film of saliva which stretched between
her lips, as if by this simple act she might deny my presence.
Even when the bubble did not catch she continued through
the motions, forming her mouth into a perfect circle, at once
seductive and defiant. She looked up, caught my stare and
began to laugh, instinctively at first, then childishly, and then
maliciously.

She left me, moving in a wide circle through the debris to
avoid the others.

That night the first of the storms arrived. It was on that
occasion that the gull had been blown against the tower,
crashing unseen and unheard, its neck broken, sliding down
the wall to wedge across the doorway.

Earlier, the other birds had risen from the sea and from the
site, moving inland in low, broken formations, passing unnoticed above our heads in their silent, effortless flight.

The bulk of the demolition work was completed. For the
majority of the men, the lorries which arrived to take them to
Lincoln would not return them to Cable Point. We said our
farewells as we waited. It was a brief, awkward ceremony,
buoyed only by their relief at the completion of the task and
their approaching return to civilian life.

My own stay would last another week, during which time I
would be largely alone, preparing to hand over the site and
awaiting my own uncertain transfer. I envied them their
certainties and the decisions being made for them.

I stood on the road, waving until the lorries disappeared, the sound of singing and shouting hanging in the warm air long after their departure. The women, too, came to say their goodbyes, wishing the men well and then gathering to discuss what was now likely to happen.

During the following week I saw very little of either Mary or her parents. It is strange, but even after having made the effort, I can remember neither of their names, knowing them simply as her mother or father.

Without his daily audience the man became subdued, appearing only briefly in the doorway, retreating from even the most casual contact. The disease which lingered to irritate the skin of his hands and face had grown worse, and he now bled at the slightest touch. The doctors in Lincoln bandaged him, and on the few occasions that I did see him, the coverings on his cheeks were bloodstained. The pain from these alone must have been unbearable. His gums, too, continued to bleed, and he no longer wore the false teeth. I knew then that if he was to stand a realistic chance of even a partial recovery, he should be committed to hospital. In the space of only a few days both his physical and nervous deterioration was clearly evident.

One evening I watched as he entered the ruins of the cleared site. He sat and began to gently rock backwards and forwards, speaking to himself and turning constantly to look towards the houses.

I learned from Donald Owen that the nightly shouting had become less frequent, but that when it did occur it was often more violent and no longer confined to the woman alone. The bruise on his wife's forehead returned, and on Mary's arm I saw a yellowing weal.

Without the daily routine and noise of the men, the growing tensions and uncertainties of the inhabitants became much more tangible, expressing themselves in anxious and resigned glances. The children, too, seemed quieter, abandoning the site and returning to play among the dunes or on the open ground beyond the Light.

As I worked at my table I heard someone by the door. I saw no one, but knew that he had been there watching me. Unexpectedly, some of my earlier sympathies for him returned: his sham of recovery had been irretrievably cast aside, and the illness which he had for so long denied was at last beginning to break him. I waited, calling his name, but no one entered.

I made a point of taking him cigarettes. His wife accepted them for him, blocking my view into their home. Later I saw as she lit and held them for him, his bandaged hands frustrating his own efforts. In these small ways she maintained a vestige of power.

His return to hospital would have solved a great many problems. But everything else had been lost to him, and he now saw his refusal to return as the one remaining decision whereby he might still stubbornly assert himself.

On the occasions when Mary accompanied him on his brief walks they neither spoke nor held hands. Once, I watched as he raised his arm as if about to hit her before lowering it gently to caress her head. She pulled free of him and walked away. He made no effort to follow her, and she in turn neither waited nor encouraged him to do so. He had become vulnerable, and just as she had done with me, she began to exploit his weaknesses.

When the van arrived to take him for treatment both attendants walked with him, insisting that he came alone. Now, even their cheerfulness was forced, and they held his arms, guiding and restraining him. In his absence I tried to speak to his wife, but she avoided me, sending Mary to make excuses.

Each evening the mist returned, and with it almost complete silence. Sitting with Donald Owen, I heard shouting and then subdued crying. This, he explained, was him and not her.

'His hands,' he said. 'He can't even hit her any more without causing himself even greater pain.'

I wondered at the extent of the man's impotence, and at the force with which it fed his resentment and frustration.

seven

The traffic is quiet now, seven o'clock, and the only sounds are those of the insects, of distant neighbours opening and closing doors, moving into their gardens to enjoy the last of the day's heat. The birds have returned and the sun has fallen sufficiently to cast a strange light on the chestnut leaves, leaving them artificially dull and with shadows of a single tone. There is no wind, and in the stillness every sound is clearly audible. I hear the clock chimes of the local church, always late, always spaced as though the next note will never arrive.

I should water the dry flower beds and lift the glass of the cold frames. The lawn, too, needs cutting, its parallel stripes of dark and pale green already losing their outlines. The water in the bowl of the stone bird bath has evaporated, leaving only a thin sediment curling away from the cup in which it has formed. When we bought the house we planned to build a conservatory onto the living room – somewhere to sit, we used to joke, when we became old. That was when we thought the process to be a gradual one; when we still believed we might have had some control over its progress.

There are things I have never told her about Michael, things she will never know. She will never know, for instance, that he spent his last short leave in London instead of with us. She will never know of the girl, of the pregnancy or of the abortion. She will never know of the things which worried him – fears which he could not even find the strength to confess to me.

Afterwards, driving home from having met the girl, I tried to understand what had happened and what we might each salvage from the situation.

She had lived in a cramped and untidy flat, unprepared for his arrival, even less for mine as he introduced me, calming her with his hands on her shoulders. Later she had cried and then apologised. I tried to imagine her as my daughter-in-law. I knew then that it was not to be. She spoke excitedly of their future together; but they were her plans, not his. The abortion, I discovered, was his idea. And with it, I realised, her plans would come to nothing.

There were photographs of the two of them around the flat. Not prominently displayed like those of my father, but hidden behind books and propped against ornaments, as if by coming across them one might also discover a badly kept secret.

He spent a week with her, and during that time she made arrangements to have the abortion.

Standing here, my back to the house, eyes closed to the falling sun, I find myself wishing that I knew where the girl was, that I could re-establish contact with her. She will not come to the funeral, but she will grieve more than any of us, uncertain and alone, and without any of the comfort the ceremony itself is designed to give. And with her, I suppose, the family line is terminated.

I saw him only once more between then and his death. He shook my hand, closed his eyes and nodded. He seemed happier, more certain of himself, as though a conflict had been resolved.

Now, even the vague noises of the evening are silent, and the thrushes and blackbirds run over the lawn in short bursts only a few feet from where I stand. They freeze and stare, straining for every sound and movement, as though constantly aware of the precise moment and circumstances of their deaths. Their shadows are long, exaggerated across the grass.

*

At the inquest I met a man who introduced himself to me as the doctor responsible for Mary's father. He too seemed uncertain of what was expected of him, equally remorseful, saying little, frustrated at being unable to confess his own true feelings. He was summoned to give his testimony before me, leaving me alone in the dark room, the first of the snow already settling against the solitary window.

It was the war, of course, to which much of the blame was apportioned. The decision shamed us all, but that which everyone else was trying so hard to forget was still providing us with its convenient excuses. Even after two years, the validity of that final, absolving decision was never in doubt, never questioned.

I saw the man afterwards, standing with his hand on the door, listening to the faint echo of voices in the room behind him. He saw me and smiled. He was as helpless as I. We exchanged nods, neither of us wanting to discuss what had happened, both of us grateful for the opportunity, as professional men, of not having to.

I knew from the manner in which I was addressed by the Court, and from the way in which my answers were received, that my own testimony was taken more seriously than that of the inhabitants. They it seemed, had tended to offer unnecessary details, revealing more of their own feelings and uncertainties than of what had happened. I came to be regarded as an observer, as an impartial and dispassionate witness standing apart from what had taken place.

Looking back, it would be reassuring for me to have seen myself as being at the calm eye around which the destructive storm was beginning to build: an observer, forcibly detached from the lives and events beginning to mesh and spin towards their tragic conclusion. Or perhaps the workers and I were a part of that rising storm – possibly even its most powerful and destructive current. Or perhaps such distinctions of detachment and involvement were unimportant. Perhaps they existed simply as an excuse, as a symptom of the guilt I felt at my weakness and inability to intervene.

From the Court I drove directly back to Oxfordshire, the journey long and uncertain in the growing blizzards, clearing my mind and replacing the details of the past with the arrangements of my forthcoming marriage. The journey lasted into the night, the stark outline of snow-covered hedges and trees rising like coral out of the darkness to close over the car.

'He could have died a thousand times!' she announced proudly and melodramatically, seeing him, I supposed, through posed newsreels or the glorious wars already being fought in Hollywood.

'As many as that?' I answered, expecting my lack of interest to stop her. But she wasn't listening, only waiting for the chance to continue.

'Could've died on any day. Three years. A thousand days, see?' Easy rhetoric had become a convincing and memorable fact. It was something he had told her, convincing them both of his will to survive as he became the hero she had wanted. Having forced me into a corner from which neither doubt nor denial was possible, she walked away, happy at her small victory, beginning to run and then to skip, her momentum building until she seemed to glide over the road, barely disturbing its film of sand.

'She was always his favourite, see.' She spoke uncertainly, covering her cheek where the remains of the bruises were still evident. She was trying to explain something, but I did not know what. After avoiding me for so long, her approach had surprised me. She watched the road, awaiting the return of her husband from Lincoln.

'Always his favourite, Mary.' The thought made her smile. 'You mustn't think too badly of him, you know.' She smiled again and I tried to understand what it was she was trying to tell me. Perhaps, like Mary, she too had begun to believe what he told her as a defence against what everyone else thought, and as a desperate measure of protection against what was happening around them.

'Is he — is he all right?'

'Yes, fine,' she said quickly. 'He's stronger all the time. Full recovery the doctors said.'

'That's what he told you, is it?'

She nodded and turned away to hide her lie. After that she began making excuses. 'They said that if he could just have a bit more time before moving on . . .'

'Did they say how long?'

She shook her head, drawing attention to the mark on her cheek by stroking it. Neither of us believed in the man's recovery, but forcing her to admit it would have achieved nothing.

'I suppose the re-training centre will — '

'Mary,' she said unexpectedly, as though realising something for the first time. She turned from the road to the house, studying its dark interior. 'She was always his favourite, see. Him and her, they — '

'Is she all right?'

'Mary? Of course she is. Why shouldn't she be?' She became defensive and there was anger in her voice.

'Oh, nothing. I just — '

'She's taken to him, you know. She's never forgotten him. They were always together, him and her.' She became calmer.

'I'm sure she must be a great help to you both.'

She wasn't listening. 'He said he had a photograph of her. Said he had it with him all the time he was in the camps, took it everywhere he went. She was only a girl, then.' She paused, the excitement draining from her voice. 'He said he lost it in London: had it taken off him, he said.' She stared absently towards the horizon. I tried to decide whether the lie was his or her own.

'Said he took it with him everywhere he went. We had it done in Lincoln just after Peter was born.' She laughed. 'The things they used to get up to! Always — '

An explosion of collapsing rubble distracted us and we turned together. Above the plume of dust rose a flock of birds, crows and gulls, climbing together and then separating as cleanly as chaff from grain, black and white in opposite directions. The dust rose and then fell, moving outwards in a circle.

Watching it, she said, 'They dropped that bomb, didn't they . . .' She began to smile and then laugh – whether in gratification at the thought of the revenge exacted or at her own returning confidence at being able to remark upon the fact, I was uncertain. 'We had pictures. What sort of bomb was it? You'd know.'

Hearing her speak like that depressed me beyond all reason. The man was not adapting to them: they were becoming extensions of him. This, despite his increasing weakness, was the way in which he was beginning to reassert himself.

At the sound of the van I left her. She began to wave. She had created an illusion, and within it she had become excited at the prospect of his return.

eight

In less than an hour I will leave to collect Michael's body. Now that the time has come I am nervous, unsure also of how she will react upon my return. She is watching me, as though trying to make up her mind about something, to say or do something. Across my legs lies the map of the route I will take. She has insisted on seeing it, on knowing. I trace my finger along the coloured lines, backwards and forwards between the grey square of our home and the exposed, dotted pattern of the airfield.

She leaves me to enter the darkened room in which the coffin will rest. I follow her and wait in the doorway. I have moved a table into the centre of the room. Now I watch as she inspects and adjusts unnecessarily the drop leaves which I have fixed upright. From the mantelpiece she takes a thermometer, informing me that the temperature of the room is below that recommended by the undertaker. I take the glass rod from her, unable to read its scarlet lines. I agree with her and tell her everything is perfect. She asks if I think the table is strong enough to bear his weight. That is what she says, 'his weight'. The curtains have been drawn since yesterday, only the slenderest strip of light still visible where they do not quite meet at the centre, where they have never quite met. She adjusts these, too, but cannot succeed in blocking out the light completely.

I hold her arms and move her towards the door. She tenses and begins to protest. I tell her that we should leave the room and not allow the warm air from the rest of the house to circulate. She says that I am right and is the first to leave. As I pass her she looks inside and smiles.

She will be alone during my absence. The aircraft will arrive at one, and from two onwards she will know that I am late and begin to worry. She asks me if there will be any speed restrictions imposed upon the van carrying the body. I suggest that she is confusing it with a funeral cortege, but the remark sounds unnecessarily cruel and so I add that I, too, am uncertain, and that this will be the reason if I am late in returning. She nods, reassured, and we are both relieved at having found an excuse for the delay of which she is already convinced. Tomorrow the house will fill with the polite grief and condolences of the remainder of her family.

Above us, a solitary fly fills the room with the insistent sound of its flight. She watches it, mesmerised, following its path between us. On the table is a small air-freshener in the shape of a rose. She lifts it, smells it, and replaces it without speaking.

Two of the younger children stretched the dead gull to its full span, running with it along the road and making the noise of aircraft. The body swung from side to side, the feathers becoming displaced and coming out in the boys' hands. One of them released his grip and the bird fell to the ground. The others gathered around it with looks of disgust, as if by falling the gull had ruined their fun. Each plucking handfuls of the long wing feathers they left it and climbed the path leading into the dunes.

An hour later the body was gone – either reclaimed by the children or dragged away by one of the cats.

Later in the day I saw their display of skulls spread along a wall. There were the pebble-sized skulls of mice, and larger ones which I thought to be those of rabbits, but which I later realised to have belonged to the cats. The children watched as

I inspected their collection, holding them up for me to examine and touch, and demonstrating the articulation of jaws where both halves existed.

Mary's shout was followed by one from her father.

The children exchanged worried glances and the older boys began hurriedly to scoop the skulls back into the tin from which they had been taken. When this was done they ran from the rear of the houses towards the shingle. Only Mary's small brother remained, watching them, uncertain of what was happening, of whether he should follow. He began to cry, and as I knelt to comfort him he too ran off, pleading for the others to wait.

The man shouted again, his words followed by a cry — whether from Mary or her mother I could not tell.

Donald Owen appeared at his rear door. 'Did you hear it?'

I nodded as I ran to join him. Together we watched the shadowed window. A face appeared and the shouting resumed.

'Is it her, or Mary?'

I told him I thought they were both in the house with the man. We continued watching the window, embarrassed and frustrated by our powerlessness.

'Do you think she's in any danger from him?'

He shrugged.

We waited for a few minutes more, but there was no further sound.

'Come away,' he said, walking towards the lighthouse.

The few men who remained sat beside the road. They too had heard, watching us and waiting for my explanation. Their own friendly gestures towards the man had long since ceased. They rose and came towards us. It was the first time anything like this had happened during their presence at the site, and the incident clearly worried them.

'Should we go and see?' one of them asked. The others nodded and threw the tea from their cups into the sand. Another suggested contacting the hospital. None of them realised the full extent of the problem or that such outbursts had once again become a regular occurrence.

As we left them they continued to discuss what had happened, their sympathies with the woman, and angry, I suspect, at my refusal to intervene

In the lighthouse Donald Owen sat down, banged his fists against the table and apologised. 'He shouldn't be here,' he said. 'It's as simple as that. He's worse than he ever was.'

'Unpredictable, you mean?'

He nodded, unwilling to add anything that would emphasise our own feelings of guilt and helplessness.

Midway between the inquest and home I passed a line of parked military vehicles, their exhausts filling the darkness with clouds of white, their headlights shining through the falling snow, creating tunnels around which it spun. At the head of the column I was waved to a halt. There had been an accident, making it necessary for me to drive on the right-hand side. Ahead of me the road stretched solidly white, broken only by the weaving pattern of the lorries. I drove on, anxious as the snow piled against the windscreen and slowed the wipers. Overhead, the naked trees met, their branches closing and providing a small measure of protection from the blizzard which raged over the surrounding fields.

There were more men, this time with lights at their feet. I saw where the treads of one of the lorries had spun across the road, and the vehicle itself, nose-down in a ditch. A second lorry lay on its side, its headlights illuminating the cab of the first. A man came forward and waved me on. Beside the lorries stood a group of young soldiers, pressed together, many of them trying to smoke.

Ten miles beyond the convoy the snow had not yet fallen, and the freezing sky became clear. I remember vividly the flickering stroboscopic effect of the headlights on the avenues of trees through which I drove, and the cream-coloured owl hanging above the road, its wings like gloved hands as it veered away, rising through the darkness.

A tarpaulin had been drawn across the cab of the upturned lorry, and two men stood beside it, their looks and gestures hiding its secret. Others clambered over the side of the lorry in the ditch. Illuminated by their brilliant lights, I saw the head and chest of a man being pulled from the wreckage, naked and white in the darkness, his eyes closed and mouth open as they raised him into the freezing air.

I moved unquestioningly from the war to the task of demolition at Cable Point, and from there too eagerly and expecting too much into my marriage. The processes of destruction and rebuilding were too inextricably linked and encouraged for any of us to escape their lasting effects. After six years we needed everything to have a beginning and an end, an end and new beginning, something better to work towards. We imposed an artificial order on our lives, and within it created the dangerous illusion of stability and certainty, of believing that looking back was dangerous. Like the survivors of a near and potentially fatal accident, we could not decide whether to laugh or cry. And just as I had hoped to find some kind of release at Cable Point after the war, so I looked forward to the securities and certainties of married life to erase my feelings of guilt and shame following Cable Point. That, I suppose, became my biggest self-deception. I became adept at creating excuses for myself – for what I had or hadn't done – and then at believing them. Our marriage stood as little real chance of succeeding as the war had done of ending with an announcement in the newspapers and dancing in the streets. We had confused hardship with genuine suffering, and then the expected dying tremors of the past with its lasting reverberations.

Years later, I often thought about the inquest and the months at Cable Point, and it seemed to me then that everything had taken place in another world, in a state of limbo almost, which had no bearing on the years which preceded or followed it. Another delusion, excuse.

It was not until several days after the shouting incident, the day after the storm, that I saw Mary again. She sat at the edge of the excavations where a narrow drain formed a boundary with the adjoining fields. Once again, columns of black smoke rose from the distant horizon, levelling to form clouds. I looked down at her from the second-floor window of the Light. She was alone, and as I watched I saw her tremble and hold herself, as though she was crying.

She had become increasingly subdued, and it seemed to me as though the remnants of her childhood were being finally discarded, leaving a vacuum into which the first assertive mannerisms of adulthood had not yet been drawn.

I approached her from behind, purposely knocking over a pile of rubble to announce my arrival. She heard, but did not turn; instead she sat upright, raising a hand to her face. I stood beside her.

'It's a lovely evening. Warm.'

She looked towards the sea and the waiting mists. 'All right.'

Her eyes were red, with pale lines down her cheeks, but I pretended not to notice.

'How are you? We haven't had a chance to chat for – '

'Chat?'

'Well, we don't seem to bump into each other so often.'

'No, I suppose not.'

'You've got a lot to do, I suppose.' I wanted to avoid mentioning her father directly. She turned to look towards the houses, anxious, as though he were behind us, watching. Squares of yellow shone through the fading light.

'Is it how you thought it would be?' It was the one question I was unable to resist asking.

She hesitated before shaking her head and looking back down into her lap. I sat beside her and she made no effort to move away.

'He seems a bit better,' I lied.

She nodded, and I wanted to console her.

'He's bound to rely on you a lot, you know – especially now. But when things get better – '

'He tells lies,' she said suddenly. 'He said it wasn't a

desert island, only a jungle. He said it was sandy, like here.'

I almost laughed. That such an unimportant detail should upset her was somehow reassuring. 'Perhaps he wanted you all to think it was a desert island so that you wouldn't be worried.'

She shrugged, unconvinced, forcing me to continue his deceptions.

'Is he like he was before he went away?'

'Sometimes. When he's not . . . He said that when we go to Lincoln we can all have new clothes. He's got a lot of money that the Army owes him. When he gets it we can all go to Lincoln.'

'I'm sure you will.'

She shrugged again.

'Don't you believe him?'

She refused to be drawn.

'How's your mother?'

'He says she worries about things too much.'

'And what does she say?'

She shook her head. I watched her closely, wondering what had caused her to cry.

'She wanted him to go and see about that place where he could work.'

'And will he?'

'Not now.'

After that we sat in silence, watching the red of the lower sky fade to grey. I gave her some cigarettes – more to re-establish the bonds between ourselves than because of what she might achieve by giving them to him. Turning to me she reached for my hand and held it, forcing her fingers between my own. She made no other advance and I did nothing to discourage her.

Looking down to where her legs hung, she said, 'He said that you told him he could get a job at the new coastguard.' There was neither hope nor disbelief in her voice.

'He told you that?'

She nodded.

'And do you believe him?'

She shrugged.

'I didn't tell him that, Mary.'

'I know.'

'Then you don't believe him?'

She nodded again.

'Why did he say it? Do you know?'

'He said it last night. He said that we'd get one of the new houses they're going to build, and that we'd have twice as much space, and a garden.'

'But you don't believe him?'

'No.'

'You won't, you know – the house and job, I mean.' I felt her grip tighten and then relax.

'No, I know. *She* believed him, though. She said that you'd been good to us and that he should – ' She stopped. I laughed and she smiled. 'Then they had a row,' she continued, releasing my hand.

'I'm sorry.'

'It doesn't really matter.'

I wanted to tell her that it did, but that things might get better. Instead, I left her and walked alone through the growing darkness to the Light. From the door I saw the leading edge of the mist roll over the shingle and approach the houses.

nine

There is more traffic than I had anticipated and I will be late in returning. The aircraft arrived as scheduled, but there was a delay caused by a missing document. The box was rectangular and not coffin-shaped, alloy instead of wood, and with only a series of meaningless numbers stencilled across its lid in white paint. The men who unloaded the remainder of the small cargo slid the box onto a collapsible trolley. I watched them, uncertain of whether or not to identify myself. After a brief discussion, one of them turned and pointed to me. I half raised my arm and they moved towards me, discarding their cigarettes as they came. A van moved between us, the driver waving his baton of release documents still to be signed.

I have already been separated from the van on two occasions, and each time I have parked and waited anxiously for its reappearance. There are no restrictions on the speed at which they may travel, but perhaps – as with the funereal pace of the men with the trolley – they feel obliged to travel slowly out of respect. They have the address but are uncertain of the route. Perhaps if I was not leading them they would drive more quickly.

At one junction I waited for them beside a telephone kiosk, and decided to ring her and explain the short delay. I dialled the number before realising I had no suitable coins. The receiver was lifted, followed by her voice. I waited without speaking, cursing my stupidity at having tried to contact her, at what she would now be thinking.

At the airfield I enquired about his belongings, but no one seemed certain of their whereabouts. They assured me of their eventual return and, being unwilling to delay any longer, I insisted that we leave without them. This, too, will cause her to worry, as will the metal box with its insensitive and cryptic stencilling.

I see her at the window. She is waiting, one hand to her face, the other holding back the curtains. People on the street stop and watch. I want to explain to them what has happened, but when they see the box they disperse. I wave to her, but she too is watching the box as the two men slide it from the van.

The nearest church to Cable Point stood six miles away at Walsham village, its squat tower visible from the lighthouse, its golden-orbed weather vane flashing when it caught the sun. It stood on a low mound at the centre of the village, surrounded by its centuries-old gravestones, all of them leaning away from the simple building, as though blown outwards by an ancient explosion through which the church had come into being. Amid the illegible slabs stood the smaller black and white memorials to those still dying in the village. It was to this church that the inhabitants of Cable Point came to be christened, married and buried.

I drove past the church following my return to the Point, after visiting the new station and seeing the dogs, the line of chalets and the woman watching from behind her lifted curtain. In the porch a memorial had been set into the wall. On it were engraved the names of the American aircrew killed whilst stationed at Walsham. Over two hundred were listed; I doubted whether there were that many stones in the graveyard. Around the memorial thumbprints of grey lichen had already taken hold, welding the violent and distant deaths of these strangers to the slow and certain, living and dying pace of the village.

I studied the mound from the car. Alongside the church I saw the newer graves, their small plots kept clear of the weeds and grasses which covered those where no family remained to tend them. I looked no closer, unwilling to know for certain which was hers, content simply to have returned and satisfied my curiosity. Perhaps if the rain had let up I might have visited the grave and inspected its glib message of loving or remorse, its colder details of beginning and end.

Through the rain, the church looked cold and uninviting, warning of its function rather than celebrating it. I knew then how little comfort it had ever been to the inhabitants of Cable Point, and how their need for it had been worn away by their generations of isolation. It had abandoned them just as completely as they now had abandoned their homes.

I awoke to the smell of burning. It was early evening and I had fallen asleep at the table, the charts and plans scattered around me. The temperature had fallen considerably since late afternoon, and with the dusk and approaching mist it was already dark.

The door remained open, and amid the ruins and rubble I saw that several fires had been started, fed with timber by the men and women who stood around them. The men pulled the wood from the debris, and the women stood together, laughing loudly and holding their exposed arms to the flames. The moving mist had already crossed the road and was seeping over the broken ground towards them. I watched unnoticed from the open doorway.

The act of lighting the fires made me uneasy: it was almost as though in the absence of myself and the others the inhabitants of Cable Point were finally reasserting themselves over the land they considered their own; as if, in the wake of the war and the site's destruction, they were reclaiming the land to use as they pleased.

The women became outlines against the flames, and in the surrounding darkness I heard their husbands, their shouting voices and the clatter of thrown bricks. The fires exploded in fountains of sparks and embers as they were fed, those standing around them applauding the effect. I searched for Mary, but neither she nor her parents were present. As the fires burned down or collapsed the men and women gathered around a solitary blaze, turning only to watch the mist as it obscured their homes and the line of the road, cutting them off. They shivered, feeling its moisture on their arms and faces, complaining as it began to smother the flames, and erupting unexpectedly into further sudden bursts of laughter. I tried to understand what was happening and what the fires meant to them.

For a while the heat from the small blazes seemed to hold back the mist, but gradually it closed over them and they were left to die, their smoke hanging low in the water-laden air.

The figures dispersed, and it was not until they moved into the dull squares of light cast by the houses that I saw them again. Following what appeared to be a brief conference, two of the men approached Mary's door and banged heavily, shouting her name and then her father's. No one answered. Undeterred, they moved to the curtained window, through which an outline of light shone, and shouted again. Others called them away, and after a second brief discussion the men withdrew. The ensuing silence was broken by a succession of loud farewells as they dispersed and returned to their own homes.

At nine Donald Owen arrived to invite me to spend the remainder of the evening with him. I accepted, grateful for the opportunity of some conversation and an explanation of what I had witnessed. I pointed to the smouldering fires as we walked. By then the mist was thick enough to obscure even the outline of the tower at a distance of twenty yards. We stood at his door, both of us searching for signs of movement on the site.

I asked him about the fires.

'Nothing to worry about. A last fling, you might call it.'

'Or the last flex of a dying muscle?' My thoughtlessness made him angry and he turned away. I apologised.

'No need,' he said, coming from the kitchen with two glasses. 'In a way I suppose you're right.'

'I thought perhaps they might want to salvage some of the timber to burn in their own homes.'

He smiled and shook his head.

'They feel that strongly?'

Again he refused to be drawn, caught, I suspect, between wanting to explain and betraying the confidences of his neighbours. He poured drinks and threw coal on to the fire, spilling ashes into the hearth where they cooled and powdered. Through the wall came the sound of something being thrown or dropped. I saw him tense, waiting. He twisted the dials of his radio, smiling to himself as the noise grew to fill the silences of our conversation.

'Was Mary at the fires?'

He said that she had been.

'And him?'

He shook his head, reluctant to discuss the event any further. Our conversation became strained. Perhaps he believed me to be interfering, knowing that whatever happened none of it would be my concern or responsibility. I *was* concerned – for Mary's sake I was concerned – but I could not admit it to him without sounding as though I was making excuses, justifying my desire to know.

'You're wrong, you know,' I said, knowing he understood what I meant. 'You all are.'

'Perhaps.'

After that he began to speculate on his own future. He showed me the letter received by each of the residents concerning the likely date of their imminent removal. He repeated the word 'likely' and laughed. Then he spoke of his return to the Merchant Navy, of his prospects and the places he intended visiting. As Mary had done earlier, he made his own departure from Cable Point sound like a great release for which he had long been waiting.

Occasionally, he moved to stand by the adjoining wall, listening.

'There's been nothing for the past few days,' he said, worried by even this lack of contact between himself and the woman.

'Have you spoken to her since – ?'

'No, no, I haven't.'

Again, I regretted having asked, having forced him to admit to something he had tried for too long to deny.

'Perhaps the doctors have finally – '

'It's got nothing to do with the doctors!' he interrupted angrily, stopping abruptly to listen to the silence which followed.

'No, of course not. I'm sorry.'

'Too quiet,' he said to himself.

I wanted to relieve the tension by accusing him of being melodramatic, of over-reacting; instead I agreed with him, and we waited.

A few minutes later the silence was broken by the sound of a slamming door, banging repeatedly as if in echo. He rose to look through the window, shaking his head as though knowing what he would see. I waited, expecting to hear a knock and for the woman to enter. As I rose to stand beside him he turned and held his arm across my path. In the darkness I saw nothing, not even the dying fires, only the reflection of my own inquisitive face staring back.

As we returned to our seats, the door slammed again. In the silence it became an explosion, a peal of rainless thunder, a demolition charge. There might also have been voices, running feet, the same few words shouted over and over, and in the mist a movement, curling and resettling. The roosting gulls rose screaming from the site, their strenuous attempts to get airborne like the applause of a scattered audience, their cries the noise of a distant playground.

He made no attempt to return to the window, draining his glass and holding a hand over his face. I swore at him and pulled open the door, searching the darkness, but seeing only the lights of the other houses and hearing only the last of the birds as they rose in a sheet into the mist.

An hour passed, and having neither seen nor heard anything else, I rose to leave. He insisted that I remain, producing another bottle, anxious that I should not leave him.

Later, when I prepared to leave for a second time, he made no attempt to stop me. Instead he thanked me for staying, and at the door he shook my hand, moving back into the room as I let myself out.

At the road I waited, only his own light and that of his neighbour still showing. From the latter I heard the subdued sound of someone crying, and needing to satisfy my curiosity and find an explanation for what had happened, I moved along the wall and looked in through the small window.

In the cramped interior sat Mary's mother and her husband. He was kneeling before her on the floor, his face buried in her lap. Beside him lay an overturned chair, pieces of broken crockery and a bunch of cloth dragged from the table. He was crying, sobbing convulsively like a small child. She cradled his head with both hands, pressing him to her, stroking his hair and soothing him. She, too, was crying, her face resting on his thin arm, rocking him gently and whispering to him. As I watched, his back arched and fell, and she held his shoulders, absorbing his convulsions and shaking violently at the effort. After a few seconds they subsided together and he once again lowered his head into her lap. Her hands were stained with blood from where his mouth and cheeks had bled. He raised his arm to touch her legs, and she moved them together for him to hold. She spoke to him and he trembled, forcing his face deeper into her lap. She folded herself over him and resumed stroking his hair, watching closely as it moved through her fingers.

I withdrew, uncertain of what I had witnessed, more anxious than ever at what might have happened, but certain now that all hopes of a recovery had finally been denied him. And I knew also that because of the hold he had re-established over his wife and children, they too were unlikely ever to recover from the trauma of his return, and that whatever had happened previously or what might now follow, tonight marked the point at which they too must have abandoned all hope of any improvement – either in his condition or in their future life together.

From the upper room in which the empty light cradle stood, I looked back over the bed of mist, seeing only the roofline of the houses with their undisturbed columns of smoke. Higher up the brighter stars were visible, and the blackness of the night where the clouds thinned and broke. I saw also the outlines of the birds as they rose and fell in effortless circles. I wondered what had disturbed them, and what now prevented them from resettling. Occasionally, they dropped into the mist and disappeared completely, feathering its upper edge as they resurfaced. Seeing them unsettled me further and I closed the window. Out at sea an invisible ship sounded its siren in four drawn-out warning groans.

I slept uneasily, and awoke to the unexpected noise of several engines and strange, shouting voices.

Beyond the houses stood an ambulance, beside it two anonymous black cars and a group of uniformed policemen. The residents stood in another group where the dunes met the road, the men and women standing separately. I searched and then shouted for Donald Owen. Everyone turned. He appeared in the doorway of Mary's house, waved to me to remain where I was, and ran to join me. At the dunes one of the women started crying and the others gathered around her, watching and comforting her, the men embarrassed by her outburst.

'What is it? What's wrong?'

'It's Mary – ' He caught his breath and was interrupted by a piercing whistle, at which the policemen spaced themselves along the road and began to move into the rubble. Some of them probed with canes, disturbing the piles of loose brick. Several others ran past us into the lighthouse and reappeared at the collar of glass. At the far end of the site the gulls rose again from their roosts and hung above us in a confetti of white against the pale sky.

'Mary – ?'

'It's him.' He closed his eyes and nodded towards where the ambulance stood.

'Is he – I – ?'

'They've sedated him. There's a constable in with him.'

'And her mother?'

As we spoke the woman appeared in the doorway from which he had emerged. He turned to watch her, anxious that she should come no further. He pointed to her and beckoned to the other residents, none of whom moved to help her. He swore beneath his breath.

As she emerged into the light, I saw that she held her young son in front of her, her hands on his shoulders. The boy was crying, but she seemed not to notice. One of the women started towards her but was called back by the others.

'What about Mary? You said – '

He pushed his palm to within a few inches of my chest.

'Stay out of it,' he said quietly, looking down to avoid my face.

'What?'

'You're not a part of all this. You never were. Leave it.'

'But surely I – '

'Leave it!' This time he shouted, and I knew not to persist, that what he was saying was causing him too much pain to have to repeat.

'And them?' I motioned towards the others.

He shook his head without looking up. In the silence which followed all that could be heard was the small boy's crying and the noise of the birds above us. It was only then that I began to make the connection between what was happening now and what I had heard and seen the previous evening.

'Mary . . .'

He nodded. 'Mary.'

Behind him the line of uniformed men gathered, realigned themselves and continued their search.

I looked to where the other residents waited. Upon my arrival I had credited them and their hard-faced fishermen and fishwife ancestors with the stubborn implacability of Red

Indians. Now, watching them, silent, subdued and unwilling to become involved, they looked like little more than the pathetic and defeated remnants of a tribe being shifted from one worthless reservation to another.

'Mary,' I repeated uselessly, and he flinched as though I had physically struck him.

At the houses the small boy pulled free of his mother, ran a few paces from her, stopped and walked slowly back.

Two policemen moved to stand on either side of her. She allowed them to hold her arms and lead her through the empty garden. A moment later she began to scream, the pitch of her voice rising with each drawn breath and final realisation of what had happened. The small boy remained in the doorway, covering his ears at the sound.

'Do they know – I mean are they sure – ?' I was still unwilling to have confirmed or to admit to believing what he had suggested.

'They know!' he said angrily, and turned away from me.

There was a second piercing whistle, and at the centre of the site the policemen moved together into a circle. He left me and ran towards them. The ambulance moved closer to the houses, and beyond it the sea caught the rising sun and exploded in a plane of blinding light.

At his arrival the policemen moved apart, and then away. He knelt to the ground, and after pushing aside some obstruction, lifted Mary's body from the rubble, balancing her across his arms and holding her to his chest as he carried her back to the road. She wore the same red dress she had always worn, her head over his elbow, her arms swinging like empty sleeves, her legs thin and white where the material had been drawn back to expose them. Then, stopping, he raised her weightless body to the level of his head, arms outstretched, and offered her to every one of us, a sacrifice to all our weaknesses. I closed my eyes, but the outline of their cross remained imprinted against the growing light. I repeated her name over and over, audibly at first, and then silently, uselessly, over and over and knowing then what I had somehow known all along, opening my eyes and watching as the gulls descended around him and disappeared into the ground.

She is with him now, alone in the darkened room, sitting beside him. The men insisted that a flag be left, and this she has unfolded, pulling its edges to the floor, smoothing it over him. It hides the metal box, making it appear much larger and more solid than it actually is. In an hour the funeral director will arrive, and he too will probably say something about the flag, about its dignity.

From where I sit I hear the occasional sound, footsteps, individual words. She is talking to him, moving around him as though in ordinary conversation. She pulls at the curtains in an attempt to eliminate the strip of brilliant light which cuts across the shadowed room with the intensity of a laser, laughing gently, as though at an amusing remark.

She thanked the two men, and they in turn told her how sorry they were. She asked if either of them had known him. They apologised again and exchanged nervous glances. I intervened, suggesting that they were already behind schedule. Both were grateful for the opportunity to leave. She has not yet remarked on the absence of his belongings.

I understand now that it is not important that my own grief has not been exhibited and shared; what does matter is that I have been able to absorb some of her own, that in her feelings for me it has been given a tangible focus, and that, unlike my own, it has been expelled. My involvement is not as passive as it might seem – simply an extension of the role I was forced to play in maintaining and supporting his necessary deceptions when he was alive. I think it is because she now realises this that her own reactions have become subdued.

I stand beside the french windows, listening, looking out. It is still warm, and the same pools of shadow ring the trees. The birds continue to run nervously between the light and dark, sifting every movement and sound for the ones to which they must devote their entire attention. The soil around the stone flags is turning to powder, and the tight roses have opened untidily and started to die. Like the lines demarcating our own divisions, the stripes of the lawn continue to blend into a single colour.

I will never know if he intended to desert, or if he had simply become dangerously careless. And the Army, in support of its own policies, will never let me know: his death has become nothing more than the cliché of an empty heroic gesture, still dressed to serve their purpose.

She closes the door gently and comes to stand beside me. I nod towards the garden and stand aside to let her see. She has been crying, her eyes dark and lined. She takes a deep breath, as though about to speak. I am outwardly calm, but I, too, can think of nothing to say. I want, instead, to hold her and for her to talk, to tell me what is happening.

It has come to this. Everything I knew, all the certainties of my life are falling away. I feel exposed, too old to draw them back around me. I have her, and that is all. Thirty-two years have passed, and a second storm has gathered and died in the spaces around me.

A flock of starlings passes overhead, their hundred fleeting shadows like blown leaves across the lawn.